A Bellwether Christmas

By Laurel Guillen

A Novel Inspired by True Events

FIDELIS
PUBLISHING

Fidelis Publishing®
Sterling, VA • Nashville, TN
www.fidelispublishing.com

ISBN: 9781956454086
ISBN: (ebook) 9781956454093
A Bellwether Christmas
A Novel Inspired by True Events
Copyright© 2022 Laurel Guillen

Order at www.faithfultext.com for discounted books. Email info@
fidelispublishing.com to inquire about bulk purchase discounts.

Cover designed by Diana Lawrence
Interior designed by Lisa Parnell
Edited by Amanda Varian
Illustrations by Cortney Skinner

Manufactured in the United States of America
10 9 8 7 6 5 4 3 2 1

To my son,
and all his wonderful animal friends.

Chapter One

Now *this is something!* thought Bart, standing on his hind legs and peering through the woven branches of the pen. Ground fog hid much of the river valley spreading out beneath him. The rising sun's rays made the mist look like a large white lake. The dark gray Apennine Mountains to the east seemed to float on it. He was only six months old and such misty weather was new to Bart. It was cold, but his thick lamb's wool kept him warm. As he landed on all fours with a little *huff,* something that looked like mist came out of his mouth. Nana, the old milk goat, opened one eye and glared at him. He darted across the pen to his friend, Ginevra, who was just waking up and stretching out her pretty legs.

"Get up, Ginevra! Get up!" he said to her. "This cold is so much fun. Watch this!" and he made more mist come out of his mouth.

Ginevra was not in any hurry to rise. "Yeah," she said, yawning, "well, watch this," and snorted loudly. Out came a little cloud. They both laughed.

It had been just a few weeks since the flock of two dozen sheep plus a few goats returned from their summer pastures in the mountains. They were back in the little farm settlement which lay smack in the middle of the boot-shaped land of Italy. The nights grew cold and the heavy rains of fall were well underway. Winter would be here soon. From now until late spring the flock would graze fields and pastures in the warmer valley and spend their nights in the sheep pen. The round pen and stable were set inside a common pasture.

Bart heard three village men talking to each other as they came through the pasture gate at the upper end. They passed by the sheep pen on the way to the stable. He couldn't make out what they were saying to each other. But from their tone of voice he could tell they were relaxed and calm.

Bart didn't want to miss anything, so he left Ginevra and trotted back to the pen's fence to have a look. He never just walked when he was headed somewhere. Why do that when trotting was faster? It made his black and white ears bounce up and down but he didn't care. Bart got up on his hind legs again and peered toward the stable. He saw a large white ox standing patiently as two of the men hitched him up to a wagon. A well-mannered brown donkey was brought out of the other stall by the third man. First a quilted pad and then some wooden supports and baskets were tied to her back. The men led the donkey and the ox and wagon past the sheep pen and out the pasture gate.

Bart went back to waiting. He nibbled at the gate latch and turned in circles. Finally, a sleepy-eyed Mundo stumbled out of the small shepherd's hut attached to the stable. The year 1223 was eventful for Mundo. His grandfather died that past winter. Just like that, at the age of thirteen, Mundo became the little village's only shepherd and goatherd. For that matter, he was its oxherd and donkeyherd too. Now this boy, who had just turned fourteen, slowly made his way to the sheep pen, one foot dragging a bit, as always. The brown curls on his head were as thick as a sheep's fleece. Every day he seemed a little taller to Bart. He already did a man's work and soon he would be as tall as a man. Bart saw him shiver under his cloak.

Mundo opened the gate of the pen and Bart was the first one out, running across the common pasture. He was followed closely by Ginevra.

"Let's jump!" said Ginevra. It was one of the games they loved best. They ran side by side and together they hopped over a boulder, then a clump of weeds and finally over the stump of the old oak tree. It was as high as their shoulders and wider than a lamb was long.

"That was fun!" said Ginevra as the two slowed down to a trot.

"I wish I could jump as high as you can," said Bart.

"Oh, you will someday," said Ginevra. "You're already as big as I am."

Bart had an idea. He spotted Peco, the flock's guard dog, laying on the slope facing the weak sun, head on his paws, waiting for Mundo. Bart picked up the pace and left Ginevra behind. He circled around with pumping legs.

"Watch this, Ginevra!" he shouted. He leapt over the dog's back, and heard a surprised *Wuff!* behind him as he bounded away.

"Oh!" shouted Ginevra. The other lambs and goats acted like they hadn't noticed, but Bart knew they did.

Bart was still so full of energy he felt like knocking something over. It was a feeling he got a lot lately. He was discovering just how much he *loved* to butt things. He was even making a list of things in his mind he liked to butt. Trouble was, there weren't many good choices. Peco was not on the list, because even though he was old and slow, he did have big teeth and a loud bark. Neither were the goats because they all had horns. Bart didn't have any horns, so he decided that really wasn't a fair contest. The adult ewes used their weight to put him in his place if he tried to butt them. The lambs who were much older than he would gladly play butt-heads with him. But he was always on the losing end of those contests too.

Then there was Ginevra. She was the closest in age to him, but still a whole month older. He saw her move away and start munching on grass. He trotted up to her.

"Let's play butt-heads, Ginevra," he said. Then without waiting for her reply, he lowered his head and playfully rammed her forehead.

"Hey, quit that!" said Ginevra. "Can't you see I'm busy eating right now? Let me have my breakfast first, please."

But Bart was just getting started. He stepped back and hit her again, and then again, a little harder each time.

Ginevra lifted her head. Suddenly her floppy white ears were no longer floppy. She thrust them backward and slightly up in the air. Bart thought they looked like bird wings, only one was higher than the other. It was a crazy look she got only when she was angry, he realized, a little too late. Ginevra's neck tensed, and then—BOOM—she hit Bart's shoulder hard. He had to scramble not to fall. That would have been bad. Falling made Bart feel helpless and scared, especially if he fell onto his back. Then he might not be able to get up easily. Besides that, Bart knew the other lambs would tease him about it for days. He might have caught up to Ginevra in size, but he had to admit she was never going to be a pushover.

Bart decided to leave hungry Ginevra alone and wandered back toward the pen to see what was keeping Mundo. Bart knew it was about time for the boy to lead the flock to

some hillside or better yet a hayfield that had just been har-
vested. They would fill their bellies all day on the remaining
stubble.

When Bart trotted up to Mundo, the boy smiled at
him. "Hey there, Bart," he said. "How are you doing today?
Getting used to the pen and the pasture?"

Bart tossed his head in reply.

Mundo was scrubbing the trough in the pen before
filling it with fresh water from the well. He also brought a
shovel and rake with him to pick up the sheep droppings
and haul them to the big manure pile. There they would
slowly rot and turn into good plant food. He left the shovel
and rake leaning against the fence. *Ah—the shovel and the
rake!* thought Bart as he sniffed them. Bart was shy around
these tools at first. But now they were more familiar. He
decided they were the perfect things to add to his list. *They
are no match for me*, he thought, tensing his neck. First, he
slammed into the shovel, then the rake. Each one fell over
with a pleasing clatter, and lay still, totally defeated. *Two
down*, he thought. *That ought to impress Mundo!*

He was very fond of the shepherd boy. Bart was the
last lamb born in the spring, and his mother died a week
later. He cried for his mother, then wandered from one ewe
to another, but none of them would let him nurse. He was
a small lamb to begin with and soon grew weak from lack
of milk. The next thing he knew, Mundo scooped him up
in his arms.

Bart remembered the boy took a piece of hollow horn
and lined it with soft sheepskin, filled it with milk and created a nursing bottle. He taught Bart to drink from the
horn bottle by holding it to the lamb's mouth while moving
Bart's tiny tail side to side, the way lambs do when they're
nursing.

"There you go, little guy," said Mundo, as Bart caught on and began to suck on the bottle greedily. He was wagging his tail on his own now. "You've got no mother anymore, so you're an orphan, just like me. But I can take care of you, don't you worry."

A few weeks later the adult sheep were sheared of their thick winter wool. Then the day came for the flock to move to the mountains behind the village. They started out mid-morning and worked their way up the trails. Bart did his best to follow Nana goat and the mother ewes with their lambs, who knew where they were going. But after climbing for almost two hours, he grew tired and started to fall behind. "Come on, Bart, you can do it," said Mundo. "It's not much farther."

Bart pushed himself and caught up where the trail leveled. But then came another climb, the steepest of all, and he felt his strength giving out. He bleated in distress as the rest of the flock moved past him. But Mundo came back for him. He squatted, grabbed him, and swung him up behind his neck and over his shoulders. Then, holding the lamb's legs with one hand, he picked up his shepherd's crook and stood up. Despite his limp, from an old injury that never healed right, the boy was a strong hiker. He managed to carry Bart as well as his leather pack full of supplies, leaning into the steep trail and digging in with the sharp end of his carved wooden staff.

In a few minutes, they reached the main summer pasture—a narrow meadow with a stream running into a little marshy pond at one end. At the other end was a sheep pen made of woven thorn branches and a shepherd's hut made of straw for shelter. From this place Mundo and Peco would guide the little flock each day to different hillsides and grassy knolls, then return them to the pen at night.

From then until fall, there were only a few times Mundo returned the flock all the way back to the settlement. Those were for the special holidays the whole farming village celebrated. On those feast days, growing boys like Mundo could eat as much as they wanted. A day or two later it would be back to the mountains, Mundo's leather pack crammed with leftover food.

Back then, Mundo still fed Bart several times a day, using milk from a ewe or Nana goat. He kept Bart tied nearby as he slept so he could feed him in the middle of the night when he got up to check on the flock. While Bart drank his milk, Mundo told him things, and the lamb listened. Pretty soon he would perk up just at the sound of Mundo's voice. Bart never forgot the things Mundo said.

One night, Bart kept Mundo company in the little shelter while the boy finished his usual meal of hard bread soaked in olive oil, fresh cheese curds, and some bean and wild onion soup. The piece of cloth usually tied across the doorway to keep the rain out was drawn back. Peco finished his portion of dinner in a few gulps and settled down in front of the hut, head facing outward, guarding Mundo and the flock. The wind finally drove the clouds away and the stars were twinkling brightly. Mundo tilted his head up to the night sky and sighed.

"Tomorrow I'll look for those berries that should be ripe by now—the red ones, your favorite, Grandpa," he said. "It feels so strange doing all these things without you. I keep expecting to hear you calling Peco or telling me not to forget to count heads every time we move. When I come back to the shelter, I keep thinking you've just gone ahead of me and I'll see you fixing the pen or adding some wild carrots to the soup pot—that you aren't really gone."

Pretty soon Mundo decided Bart didn't need the bottle any longer. The littlest lamb had a big appetite for grass and was steadily gaining weight. It helped that summer never got as hot and dry in the mountains as it did down in the village, and the grass stayed thick and green. Even so, Bart missed spending his nights inside the hut with Mundo. He looked for chances to come over to the boy and get his back scratched. Whenever the shepherd sat on a rock and took out his shepherd's pipe, Bart would move closer. To Bart, Mundo's flute playing sounded like some lovely bird, singing its heart out. Mundo would look around between songs and there would be the lamb, grazing only a few feet away.

Bart remembered one sunny day when Mundo came and sat down near him and took out the carved wooden flute from its pouch at his waist. The boy held the instrument so its open end pointed toward his feet. He blew into the mouthpiece while covering the holes to make the different notes. A breeze began to blow and Mundo let the notes of the little tune fall away into silence.

"You were so proud to be a shepherd, Grandpa," Bart heard the boy say softly. "I remember you always saying 'we are blessed to be shepherds because our Lord called himself our Good Shepherd.' Well, you were a good shepherd, Grandpa." Mundo hung his head. "Not like me."

Bart wanted to tell Mundo he thought he was a very fine shepherd. But he didn't know how, so he just listened.

"You taught me well," said Mundo. "It's just . . . it's hard watching over the flock night and day, with only Peco and the sheep for company. I'm all alone for four months—except for holidays, and once a week when one of the cousins comes here with supplies. And it's not much better in the winter, living in the hut without you.

"It's true Aunt and Uncle won't let me starve or freeze to death. Not quite, anyway," Mundo said, watching the breeze-blown clouds. "And I know if I work hard, I can have lots of sheep of my own someday. But sometimes I think I'd rather be a merchant, going to fairs and visiting busy towns all over the place. I loved it when you took me to Rieti for the fair. And when we went all the way to Terni to hear the poor preacher. If I were a merchant, I could travel as far as Rome and Milan. Wouldn't that be great!

"Better yet, I could be a minstrel—then I could eat as much as I want at rich lords' tables. I could play ballads all day long and pretty maidens would smile at me. That sounds like a great life. I know, I know, I don't have a lot of musical training. All I know are simple country tunes on this shepherd's pipe you gave me. But at least I'm getting better all the time. Maybe you were right and I do have a gift for music. Plus, I have a decent singing voice. Don't I, Bart? You like it when I sing to you, right boyo?"

Bart wagged his tail and bleated, *Baa!*

"I just wish my voice would hurry up and get deeper!" said Mundo.

It hadn't been long after that when the nights grew cool. Mundo and Peco rounded up the flock and herded them back down the mountain to the little settlement. This time, instead of lagging behind, Bart grew impatient with the slow speed of the adults. He wanted to run all the way.

"Where do you think you're going?" snapped Nana goat as he passed her while leaping from one boulder to another. "Little lambs don't lead, if you haven't noticed."

Bart pretended he didn't hear her. He kept on bounding from rock to rock out in front of everyone, while imagining all the things awaiting them at home. That's how he missed a turnoff in the trail and had to double back at a run to rejoin the flock.

"Stay with the others!" growled Peco, who appeared alongside him. So Bart held back until the flock reached the common pasture. But he still managed to be the first one through the gate.

Now on this chilly fall morning, while Mundo worked inside the sheep pen, Bart amused himself by butting a bucket, once, twice, three times. He looked around for something else to butt. The rake and shovel were still lying on the ground. Bart figured they didn't dare get up and face him again. Then he had the thought, *How about Mundo?* He nudged the back of the shepherd's leg.

"Hey!" said Mundo, who turned around and saw Bart backing up and putting his head down.

"Let's have a butting contest!" bleated Bart, as he took aim at the boy's knee.

"Bart, NO!" said Mundo sternly. Bart knew what "NO!" meant, but he charged anyway. For a boy with a bad leg Mundo shifted very quickly. Bart ended up butting a thick wooden fence post. Bart shook his head, only a little dazed. Like all sheep, he had a very hard skull.

"I can't let you do this, Bart, or you'll do it when you're bigger and that could really hurt me," said Mundo. But Bart wasn't listening. He was backing up for another try. "Alright then, but don't say I didn't warn you," Mundo called out, bending down to pick up a bucket.

"Here I come!" said Bart as he crouched and charged.

WHOOSH!

What felt like a trough full of water landed on Bart's head and halted him in his tracks. He stood there, drenched and sputtering, water streaming from his mouth and nose.

It was a shocking, nasty feeling. With a *WHIrrrrrrrrrr* he shook himself from head to tail.

Mundo was making those sounds in his throat that meant he thought something was funny. "Sorry, little guy," he said. "You remember this from now on. No butting Mundo!"

Bart felt terrible. He thought Mundo was his buddy. But this disaster changed everything.

Mundo was off his butt list forever.

Chapter Two

As the wet fall season went along, the river in the valley swelled. Its rushing, roaring sound could be heard for days after every rain. The villagers hurried to gather the last of the crops before freezing weather set in. Cabbages and lettuces were pulled from gardens. Late apples and quinces were plucked from the orchard. Any passed-over fallen or rotten fruit or nuts were fed to the pigs or eaten by the little flock when it was allowed into the orchard to nose around.

Mundo often took the flock up into the foothills just behind the village to graze. He always brought his axe, because his second job in the cold months was cutting and piling wood. Sometimes after the flock was put to bed in the sheep pen, Bart saw Mundo chopping wood under a bright moon well into the night. He looked pretty tired when he finished.

Bart was getting used to being in the village again. One thing it had the mountains didn't was a well-traveled road. Built more than a thousand years earlier by the Romans, it was the main route between the Umbria region and the Rieti Valley and went all the way to Rome. For most of the way the road hugged steep mountain walls. But at the farm settlement, the mountain walls drew back to reveal a green, sloping dale. It filled the gap in the mountains like a pretty little painting set in a rugged frame.

In the center of the dale was a large brick-and-stone storage building called the grange. It had a water well in front of it and moss-covered stone cisterns to collect the water that ran off its roof. Carved above its main doorway was the image of a castle with six towers, the seal of the Lord of Greccio.

Clustered around the grange were wooden and straw cottages built on top of stones, where more than a dozen families lived. All of them were farm workers of some sort. Some of them were good at other skills that went along with farming, like carpentry, butchering, cheesemaking, stone-laying, and bread baking. Each family had a small yard with its own vegetable and herb garden. Here and there silver green olive trees grew in clusters. Chickens and geese wandered around and pigs grunted. Further from the grange was the common pasture, the orchard, a vineyard, and some hay fields. Below the road, going all the way down to the river, were fields of grain and beans.

The sight of this little lap of land between the knees of a mountain often brought a smile to the face of people traveling the road. Sometimes they would walk up the path past the common pasture to get a drink of water from the well. Or they would rest a few minutes on the low stone wall above the road and gaze at the view across the widening river valley below. The settlement was too small to have a proper name. It was more of a hamlet or a farmstead than a village. People just called it the Grange, or Greccio Grange, since it was a part of Greccio.

Bart discovered from the high end of the common pasture that he had a good view of people and animals on the road. Peasants carried sacks or farm tools over their shoulders. Merchants headed to market leading donkeys loaded with baskets of goods to sell. With the grain harvest just ended, there were many ox-drawn carts hauling wheat and barley to the water mill down at the river. There it could be crushed into flour. Other carts hauled wine barrels or baskets of onions and garlic, or clay jars full of oil. The first day Bart started watching the road, two carriages went by pulled by fine horses. He spotted ladies inside the carriages, their white head scarves fluttering in the breeze like doves.

Yesterday, on their way back to the pasture from a day of grazing a nearby hilltop, Bart heard a rumbling noise. It was coming from the north. As they all looked to the road, a group of mounted men appeared from around the bend. Bart gawked. He knew you could tell a lot about humans from the clothes they wore and the way they got around. The horses these men rode were sturdy and wide, lifting their feet proudly. They had shiny metal on the sides of their bridles and along their foreheads. It jingled as they moved.

The riders were all heavily muscled. They wore padded clothing and some had on hooded shirts made of hundreds of small, linked metal rings. Bart noticed swords at their hips and other sharp-looking weapons tied behind their saddles. Leather gloves covered thick hands. There were banners and decorations in bright, bouncing red and blue and yellow colors. The horsemen went at a fast walk down the high middle of the road, avoiding the worst of the mud. They looked neither left nor right. A Granger who was about to cross the road to the field below stopped and bowed his head as the horsemen passed. A string of five pack mules tied together and loaded with bundles brought up the rear. In a few minutes the mounted men passed around the mountain wall at the south end of the little dale and disappeared.

Mundo was as excited by the sight as Bart. "Hey there, Bart, did you see those knights passing by? Weren't those chargers they rode really something? And that's some fine chain mail they were wearing. Did you see how big those guys were? What I wouldn't give to have muscles like that! I wonder where they are going—some place far away, no doubt!"

Bart tossed his head in reply.

Mundo and Peco put all the sheep and goats into the pen. "What do you think, Bart?" Mundo said, flexing his arms to show his muscles. "It's hard work but I think all that wood chopping is making me bigger and stronger."

Bart tilted his head sideways and stared at the lanky boy. He really couldn't tell if he was any stronger. Were they still buddies and could butt heads, he would be able to judge the matter in an instant.

Mundo laughed at Bart's expression. "Sometimes I think you understand everything I say," said Mundo. He closed and latched the gate of the pen. "Goodnight, boyo," he said, giving him a parting scratch on the back.

This morning, while most of the other animals were still asleep, Bart worked on the gate. His habit of nibbling things had paid off before. This time he managed to raise the metal loop holding the gate to the post with his nose *just so.* The sky was still darkened by rain clouds but there was a hint of dawn. He wedged his nose into the gap and pushed the gate open. Then he trotted quietly over to the stable where the ox and donkey slept.

"Good morning, Violeta," said Bart to the donkey.

"Who is that?" said Violeta in her breathy voice. "Oh, it's you, Bart. Good morning. You're up early."

"I didn't mean to startle you, Violeta," said Bart. "I was just wondering what you have been helping the villagers with lately. Is it harvesting grapes?"

"No, dear boy," said Violeta. "The grape harvest is over. We are getting the last ripe olives from the trees to make olive oil."

Bart was just getting to know Violeta and Jaco. The ox's size and strength still scared him. But he liked the donkey a lot. For one thing, she always answered his questions politely and patiently. For another, she wasn't loud like other donkeys, *HEE-HAW*-ing at the top of their lungs. When she brayed, it sounded like a gentle little inhaled breath followed by a sigh. She couldn't be heard at all if you weren't standing within a few yards.

"I hope you don't mind my asking, but why is it that you don't bray loudly like other donkeys I've heard passing by on the road?" asked Bart.

Violeta put her head down in her humble way. "I'm certainly able to bray loudly, Bart dear. But that would attract a lot of attention. I don't like to do that because it is not always a good thing. Besides, braying loudly wastes energy. I don't want to do that unless it's for something very important."

Bart thought that made a lot of sense. The silly goats were always making noises over the littlest things. "Oh, we're being let out now! *Buh-uh-uh!* Oh, there's a butterfly! *Buh-uh-uh!*" The lambs and the ewes were only slightly better.

"You're right, Violeta. From now on I'm not going to make noise without a good reason, either," said Bart.

Jaco, who was eating the last of his hay from the night before, stuck his big white head and horns out of the stall next to Violeta's. Even his black nose looked huge to Bart.

"What's up, young fellow?" he said, hay slipping out of his mouth as he spoke.

Bart gobbled up the bit of fallen hay lickety-split. It was delicious!

Jaco thought of himself as the chief of all the Grange animals. Not only was he the largest, he was also very important to the little village because of all the work he could do. Bart quickly realized talking to the ox might help satisfy his curiosity *and* his belly at the same time.

"Well, Jaco sir, I was wondering if you and Violeta could tell me about Mundo's grandfather. Mundo seems to miss him a lot."

"Mundo's grandfather was a kind person who loved animals, just like Mundo," said Violeta.

"Yes. Just like his grandfather, Mundo is never cruel. He knows when to make calm, soothing sounds, and he seems to know just where on your body you are sore," added Jaco.

"Well, I'm starting to think he doesn't really like sheep very much. When we were in the mountains I heard him say he wished he was something else instead of a shepherd. And lately he doesn't play very fair," said Bart, still smarting from the memory of his soaking.

Jaco pulled another mouthful of hay from his hay rack and swung his head back out of the stall. "He just doesn't put up with nonsense," said Jaco. "His grandfather taught him that too."

Bart gulped down the falling hay as soon as it hit the ground. Then he said. "So why do you two put up with humans?"

Jaco munched more slowly. "They are weak and need my help. I help them and, in turn, they feed me well," he said, hay dribbling from his mouth. By the time he pulled more hay from his rack, and put his head out the stall again, Bart had eaten all the fallen scraps.

"I like being helpful too. I usually do what they ask of me," said Violeta, in her soft voice. "Unless of course they want me to do something new that I haven't had time to think about, or something that's just plain foolish. And there are times they don't realize I'm so tired I'm about to collapse, and they keep asking me to work. Those are the times I'll dig in my heels and I won't budge."

"So how come humans can't always understand what we're telling them?" asked Bart.

"I don't really know," said Violeta. "Maybe it's because they think we only speak with our voices, when we speak with our whole bodies. It's puzzling, because they are in charge, but in many ways they are a lot like us. They get tired and hungry and hurt, like we do. They have little ones and they grow old, like we do. They even have masters they have to serve, like we do."

"You mean like shepherds?"

"Not exactly. Their masters are called knights, strong men who ride horses and wear metal and carry weapons."

"We saw some of those on the road just a few days ago!" said Bart.

"When knights come around, the Grangers do what they say," said Violeta. "I hear the men in armor have a master, Lord Giovanni, who lives in a castle, a big stone house with towers. I've seen it on the other side of our mountain."

She paused and spoke even more softly now. Bart moved closer to hear her better.

"Once some knights on horses came and took away some of the village sheep, geese, and chickens, two of the young men, and my beautiful son Seymour. To this day Seymour has never returned. It still makes me sad that I don't know what happened to him," said Violeta with a sigh.

"That's terrible!" said Bart. "I'm very sorry to hear that, Violeta."

"The way I look at things," said Jaco, chewing slowly as he thought. "Everyone . . . has to have . . . their place. They can't all . . . be a boss . . . like me. The strong must be in charge . . . of the weak." Bits of hay fell each time Jaco spoke.

"But you are much stronger than a human, so why aren't you in charge of them?" said Bart. As soon as he said this, he heard how sassy it sounded. He hoped he hadn't pushed Jaco too far.

"I *am* stronger!" said Jaco with a huff. "But they can gang up on you . . . with ropes and sticks . . . and they are very tricky. So it's easier . . . to do what they ask . . . and then I get to enjoy the warm stall . . . in winter and all . . . this hay they give me," said Jaco.

By this time, there was no more hay left in Jaco's rack. And Bart was gobbling up the last pieces falling from the ox's mouth.

Jaco finally noticed how much of his food ended up going into Bart's stomach. "And don't think, little lamb," rumbled Jaco, "that just because I'm so agreeable, I can't pick you up on my horns and toss you so far the wolves will get you!"

Bart skittered backward and nearly ran away.

"He doesn't mean that," said Violeta.

"What are *wolves*?" Bart asked, not liking the sound of the word.

"They're like big dogs, only much more sly, fierce, and terrible. Wolves LOVE to eat lambs if they can get them," said Jaco.

When she saw Bart tremble, Violeta quickly added, "But there haven't been any around here for quite a while. Humans kill every one they can. I've only seen wolves once, years ago when my Seymour was very little."

"Really? Around here? That doesn't sound good," said Bart.

Violeta was silent for a minute, thinking back. "Well, I remember it was late spring, a few weeks after Seymour was born. Peco, Mundo, and his grandfather, who was the shepherd back then, had just left for the mountains with the sheep and goats. I wasn't working full days because Seymour was still so small. On this afternoon we were let out into the common pasture. At dusk two young wolves came slinking down the mountainside behind the village. They were watching us from above. I charged in their direction to show I wasn't afraid. I brayed and let them know I would grab them with my teeth and shake them and stomp them with my hooves if they came any closer! Thank goodness they decided to leave and never returned."

"Wow, Violeta," said Bart. "You were so brave!"

"She was a lot louder in those days too," mumbled Jaco.

Violeta lowered her head modestly. "I would have done all those things to protect my foal," she said. "But we were lucky. It could have been much worse. Anyway, it's not something you should worry about, my dear Bart."

Bart shivered at the thought of creatures who could make calm Violeta get so worked up. Just then they heard Mundo coming out of his hut. He would have walked right into Bart if the lamb's white fleece didn't stand out in the dim dawn light.

"What!?" cried Mundo. "How did you get out? I didn't leave the gate unlatched. Did I?"

Bart was already trotting back the way he came, his black and white ears bouncing up and down. Rain started to drizzle from the sky. Mundo sighed and made his way over to the freed sheep and goats milling around outside the emptied pen. They were waiting impatiently for their shepherd to bring order to their day.

Chapter Three

The nights were growing colder, and nights without clouds were the coldest. One morning as the gray sky turned to clear blue, the flock followed Mundo and Peco to a field behind the common pasture. Under the faded green knee-length tunic Mundo always wore, his legs were usually bare. But today he was wearing woolen hose. It had patches but at least it looked warm.

Frost iced the short grass and made it crunch as Bart stepped on it. The field was once thick with grass higher than Bart's head. Now it looked like the back of a sheared sheep. At the top of the gentle slope a border of scrubby brush held back the oak and pine woods clinging to the steep mountainside. Mundo took out his small axe for chopping branches.

"Now you all stay where I can see you," Mundo told the little flock. "I've got to cut some more wood." He went to work on the brushy area, but looked up every few minutes in case any sheep or goats strayed too far.

Bart grazed his way across the field to the highest point. He stared up the mountainside, trying to see a path leading to the top of a little knoll. He remembered the wonderful breeze there and the tall grass growing between the trees. As he bent his head back down to pluck some blades of sheared-off grass stubble, something near him moved. Startled, he jumped. He was about to flee when he recognized the small furry animal, with long, dark-tipped ears. He saw a couple of this type before, but only from a distance. This one was chewing calmly on a plant, so Bart decided to introduce himself.

"Hello, small one. My name is Bart. I'm a male lamb, a wether. What are you?"

"I'm a hare," the little animal said, looking up at him. "My name is Seconda, because I am my mother's second doe this season. I'm out here looking for tasty greens. Pretty soon, when the sun is all the way up, I'll go back to my burrow to sleep."

"Well, I don't want to interrupt your meal. But I've never spoken to a hare before. I belong to the Grange flock."

"Oh, I don't belong to humans the way you do," she replied. "I live out here in the wild. I'm free to come and go as I please. Of course, hawks and wolves and dogs and lynx and weasels love to eat hares if they can catch us. Humans too. They will try to catch me or my brothers and sisters in a trap if they can."

She paused and a hind foot came up to scratch at her ear.

"I really shouldn't say all humans like to trap us and eat us," she said.

"Why not?"

"My family knows of some humans who freed a hare from a snare trap."

"Oh, really? Who were they?"

The little hare sat up, twitched her nose and whiskers, then cleared her throat, as if about to recite something from memory. She said, "Here is the story of the men who freed my grandfather from a trap when he was a young buck.

"Many summers ago, my grandfather was at the edge of a wood and heard some men coming near. They wore robes the color of a hare's fur and they were singing. He said it was a nice sound, a happy sound. They stopped not far from him and sat down in a circle. They couldn't see him, but he could see them taking something out of the pouches at their waists and eating.

"Then one of them got up to go into the woods. My grandfather decided it was time to leave and hopped away through a little tunnel of brush. But as he did, he felt a snare tighten around him. He struggled, but the noose only got tighter. He couldn't breathe. But the man who had gone into the woods saw him. He knelt and pinned my grandfather with one hand. My grandfather thought his end had come. But the man broke the string holding him, pulled it off, then lifted him in his arms. He carried him over to where the others were sitting and put him down on the grass.

"My grandfather sat there for a moment trembling with fright. Then the leader of the men said, 'Brother Hare, come here. Why did you let yourself be fooled this way?' My grandfather said as soon as he heard this man's voice, he understood him and wasn't afraid anymore. Instead of running away, he hopped over to him and jumped into his lap. While the man smiled and stroked my grandfather's fur, he spoke to the other men, calling them 'Brothers' as well. He told them 'Brother Hare' was one of their Father's creatures.

"My grandfather said he never felt so safe in his entire life. We hares never do feel safe, you see.

"After a little while, the man lifted my grandfather from his lap and set him gently on the ground. He said, 'You can go now, Brother Hare. You are free.' But my grandfather didn't want to leave and climbed back into the man's lap. Again the man gently put him down and again my grandfather climbed back up. At last, one of the other men picked him up and carried him to the woods. There, finally, my grandfather hopped behind a bush.

"He stayed hidden for a long time watching the one who stroked his fur and called him Brother. Only when the men left did my grandfather go on his way.

"From that day on my grandfather decided he would do what the kind man said and try very hard never to get trapped again. And he never did. He passed this story down to all his children and taught them how to avoid hidden snares. He taught this to my mother and then she taught me."

"That's a wonderful story!" said Bart.

"Thank you. I've never told it to a lamb before," said the hare. "It was very nice meeting you, Bart. I will be leaving now as the sun is getting high in the sky," she said.

"Very nice to meet you, Seconda, goodbye," said Bart. In the blink of an eye the hare dashed into the thick line of brush and was gone from sight.

Bart was so excited about his talk with the hare, he went to find Ginevra and the other sheep and goats to tell them all about it.

"Why do you think that man freed the hare from the trap in the first place?" Ginevra asked when he finished.

"I don't know," said Bart. "Maybe because the leader said the hare belonged to his father. I wonder who his father was?"

Bart sighed. "There sure is a lot I don't know about the world, and humans are the hardest part to understand."

Nana goat, grazing nearby, heard every word. She gave a loud snort.

"I'll tell you what's easy to understand," she said. "Humans want something from us—our wool or our milk or our meat or our work. But here's what I can't figure out. Most of the lambs born in spring become part of some rich person's holiday feast. When your mother died, Mundo's uncle wanted him to sell you for slaughter. But instead, Mundo fed you some of my precious milk and kept you alive. *Why?*

"You behave worse than any of the other lambs. And on top of that you're a neutered male so you'll never be a breeding ram. They say wethers have nicer fleeces than ewes. I don't see it in your case. All I can figure is you were lucky to be born so late."

Ginevra gave a snort of disgust. "Some goats get so old they grow mean. Probably makes their milk bitter too," she said hotly.

Bart was speechless. He knew Nana goat didn't like him much, but that didn't lessen the truth of what she said. He could have been slaughtered, like so many others, but Mundo stepped in and saved him. Why? He trotted away from Nana goat and the others to think.

Ginevra followed quietly to keep him company.

It was true he was not as well made as the others, Bart admitted to himself. He was small at birth and didn't have the perfectly straight back and handsome legs that Ginevra had. So far, his fleece *was* just average. What's more, Nana was right. He was always doing things he wasn't supposed to. He couldn't help himself! What it all came down to, he concluded, was this: he was a sheep that wasn't worth much and didn't seem to fit in. And that was a very scary thought.

❦

For the next week Mundo and some other Grangers spent the days cutting and bringing down wood from the mountainside. With the help of Jaco and Violeta, the men hauled it downhill to a spot where it would be cut up for firewood. The loads did not include any big tree trunks, because the large trees were used for lumber and could only be felled for Lord Giovanni's use. The villagers were allowed to cut only brush, dead wood, and saplings. The leafy twigs on the brush would be stored in the grange building and fed to the sheep, goats, donkey, and ox over the winter. While all this was going on, the little flock was left to roam freely around the common pasture.

Bart went to his favorite place at the high part of the pasture so he could watch the road. As he grazed near the wooden fence, he found a spot where a part of it jutted out at just the right height and angle.

Sheep tend to have itchy backs. You would too if you had all that wool next to your skin and little pieces of twigs and leaves and dirt stuck in it. Bart leaned into the fence and rubbed first one side, then the other. *Ahhhhh! What a relief!*

When the sun had nearly reached the mountains high above him, Bart heard a lark singing its happy song as it flew over the back field. It landed on the pasture fence not far from where he stood.

"That's quite a song, Mr. Lark," Bart said, not moving much so he wouldn't startle the bird.

"Yes, yes! I know winter is coming, but I can't help feeling rather cheerful all the same. My babies have grown and left the nest, there is all this spilled seed to find in the cut fields. And I'm doing what my Creator meant for me to do. I'm being a lark."

"What do you mean your Creator?" asked Bart.

"Well, you see, we birds fly around quite a bit. I have flown over the top of these mountains, and all up and down the river valley. You can see so much more when you are up in the air. Why, just a short flight north from here the river water all rushes down a steep cliff and makes a great big splash."

"I didn't know that. It sounds awesome," said Bart.

"Yes, yes, it is! As we fly all around, we larks hear many things from other birds, and other creatures—even from humans. There is one man, the Poor One, who has taught us a lot of things. Oh yes, yes, he has spoken with us many times."

Bart cocked his head to one side but otherwise stayed very still.

"Anyway, this poor man says his Father the Creator loves us birds and gave us wings, and feathers, and voices, and the pure mountain air to fly in. He says he gives us food every day, even though we birds don't plant or harvest crops. He says this Creator knows everything about us, and even knows when a little sparrow falls from the sky."

Bart was gripped by curiosity. "Did this Creator make anything else besides birds?" he asked.

"Why, why, he created EVERYTHING in the world, including all the beasts of the fields and all the herds on the mountainsides. They all BELONG to HIM. He even created YOU, little lamb!" cried the lark.

Bart thought about this amazing news. "If we all belong to him, then what does this Creator want from us? Is it wool or meat or feathers?" he asked.

"No, no! The Poor One says all we need to do is praise him and honor him by singing and flying around—by just being the birds we are. That's all. So, now, whenever I sing my song, I sing it to praise the Creator. Yes, Yes!"

Bart thought about this long and hard. "This Poor One," he said at last, "is he kind and does he by any chance wear a plain robe and wander about and sing a lot?"

"Why yes—yes, he does! He and his flock wear robes the color of a lark's feathers, but rough, like sacks, and they tie a rope around their waists. They are always moving around. The tops of their heads have no hair—it's one of the ways we can spot the Poor One from the air. He is certainly kind to us. I'd say he does sing pretty well too, for a human."

"Then I think I have heard of him," said Bart.

"He is very well known in these parts—at least he is among the birds. I am sorry you don't have a beautiful voice like a bird, little lamb. Yes, it's a pity. But maybe you can find another way to give praise and honor to the Creator who made you. Well, I must be off, goodbye now."

Bart watched as the lark flew up and away, chirping and trilling a merry song. For a while he kept grazing where he was, in case the lark came back or another bird landed on the fence.

Like any sheep, Bart had to stop eating every so often so he could re-chew his food before digesting it. To do this, he folded his front legs and kneeled, then settled his back end down. With his four legs tucked under him he began to chew his cud and go over in his mind what the lark and the hare told him. The words they used—*belong*, *love*, *honor*, and *praise*—kept repeating in his head. They sounded like very wonderful things.

When Bart was hungry again, he got up and started snapping at the grass. Like all sheep, he didn't have any top teeth in the front of his mouth, but he didn't need them. With his bottom teeth and his top gums, he could shear the grass quickly and cleanly. At last, he stopped to scratch his back along the fence again.

That's when he noticed something. At the spot where he'd been rubbing, some branches were no longer woven firmly into the fence. When he pushed on them, they bent outward easily. It became clear to him a good-sized opening could be made in the fence with a little more pushing. An opening big enough for a lamb to get through. He stored this interesting fact away for another day.

Chapter Four

Greccio Grange was busier than usual since yesterday. The air was filled with the smell of food cooking over hearths. And from early in the morning until late at night, there was the delicious aroma of baked bread. The settlement was too small to have a full-time baker, so all the families brought their dough to a little common bakehouse. It held a large brick oven and some shelves. One family was in charge of setting the fire, keeping it going, taking the loaves or baked goods out of the oven to cool when they were done, and cleaning the soot from the oven.

This morning a constant stream of people went in and out of the grange building. Men and boys brought in planks and sawhorses to make long tables. Women and girls carried in baskets and trays of food—cheeses, plates of vegetables, sausages, the usual dark flat bread but also sweet cakes and pastries, fish roasted in herbs and olive oil, and jugs of water and wine.

Mundo seemed excited as he hurried out of his hut. Bart was standing on his hind legs so he could see over the top of the pen's gate.

"Happy St. Martin's Day, Bart!" cried Mundo before he reached the pen. "Today I get to eat as much as I want. It's been a good harvest this year, so there will be lots of food." Mundo undid the latch as he talked. "I've been dreaming of sausages and almond cakes and apple fritters. And we're going to roast chestnuts around the bonfire tonight. I'll just have to make sure I don't get too full to play my flute! I've been practicing new tunes all summer. You know—the ones you like so much. Wish me luck, boyo!" he said, as he pulled the gate open.

The sheep and goats poured into the common pasture. Bart tossed his head at Mundo, then turned and trotted away to the stable, his black and white ears flopping up and down. Jaco and Violeta were relaxing in their stalls. They had a rare day off to just munch hay and take naps.

"Hello, Violeta. Hello, Mr. Jaco, uh, sir. What's happening today?" Bart asked.

"It's the last day of the fall harvest and the beginning of winter," replied Violeta. "The Grangers celebrate it every year. They will be eating and dancing and making music all day, and not even thinking about working. That's just fine with me."

"Me too," said Jaco. "If we are lucky, they won't start working again until the sun is well up in the sky tomorrow morning."

Just then Bart heard Mundo's name being called by two women, who were struggling with a large tray. Mundo, who was heading in the opposite direction, did an about-face and hurried over to help.

The lamb, the donkey, and the ox watched as people scurried here and there. Everyone, young and old, seemed happy and excited. Bart looked over at Peco, who Mundo left behind and ordered to stay put in the pasture. The dog was lying in his usual place. But every once in a while, he would get up and walk to the upper pasture gate, to sniff the air with its scent of garlic and roasting meat. He would whine and grumble to himself, then turn around, and go back to his spot by the stable. It was clear Peco would rather be at the feast with Mundo, where the fallen scraps were bound to be delicious.

"Pretty soon," said Violeta, "comes the biggest feast of all. It lasts for days and days. The villagers give each other gifts and play all sorts of games and say 'Merry Christmas' to everyone they meet. That holiday will be here very soon. We might even have a little snow by then."

"What's snow?" asked Bart.

Violeta thought a moment. "It's kind of like mist that gets so cold it turns pure white and falls from the sky," she said.

"I hope I get to see *that*," said Bart. "Now, if you don't mind, I wanted to speak with you both about some curious things a hare and a lark told me."

He told the donkey and the ox all about his talk with the two wild creatures. While he did so, the other sheep and goats drew closer as they grazed. Peco stayed where he was, lying with his shaggy head on his paws, but Bart noticed he had one ear cocked toward them in order to hear better.

"So you see," Bart finished, "it might be that the hare and the lark are talking about the same man or group of men. And these men don't seem to talk or act like other humans."

"Remarkable," said Violeta.

"Hmmmmph!" grunted Jaco.

"I'm confused about something," said Bart. "It's the part where the lark talks about 'belonging' to the Creator. What do you think it means? And the part where the poor, kind man said the hare was one of his father's creatures. So is the poor man's father the Creator?"

Violeta chewed this over for a few minutes before she spoke. "Belonging isn't easy to understand, Bart," she replied. "Take this little farmstead we live on, for instance. You might say it belongs to the villagers, the Grangers, since they work hard to grow hay and grain and vegetables and gather firewood and raise and care for the animals. But Lord Giovanni is the master of Greccio, and the villagers give him most of what they grow. Many of the spring lambs and the young pigs fattened up all summer end up on his table too."

"For his part, Lord Giovanni protects the people and makes sure laws are obeyed. That's what he has those knights for. And when there is a bad harvest, he takes less of it, so none of his people starve. I have seen starving people traveling on the road in bad times, so some lords must not be as generous as he is. Just like some people don't know how to treat animals." She added with a sigh, "I wish I knew who was taking care of Seymour."

After a moment of thought, Bart said, "Since the Creator made everybody and everything, then he must be Lord Giovanni's Creator too."

"Yes, Bart, I think you are right," said Violeta.

"So . . . that means the Creator knows him and takes care of him too. It sounds like the Creator wants all his people and all his animals watched over and protected and cared for," said Bart.

"It's just like I say, the stronger ones take care of the weaker ones," said Jaco with a proud huff.

"Those men saved that hare from dying," Bart said quietly. "Just like Mundo saved me when his uncle wanted to sell me for . . ." Bart couldn't finish the sentence.

"Yes, my dear," said Violeta. "In a way Mundo saved you twice. Once when your mother died and you needed milk, and once when he convinced his uncle not to sell you."

"Do you know *why* he did that?" asked Bart.

"No, I don't," said Jaco, not meaning to sound unkind.

"I'm not sure why," said Violeta. "But I'm certainly glad he did."

Bart's heart dropped. But he thanked them both before trudging away. It was just like Nana said. There was no good reason for Mundo to have kept him alive. It's not like he improved the village flock. He was just a useless wether.

The day wore on and Bart picked at the grass. He tried watching the road. But there were hardly any people traveling. It seemed no one was working today. They were probably having feasts of their own, Bart thought. When he settled on his folded legs to chew his cud, Ginevra came over and settled near him to do the same.

After a while he noticed the sun finished its rise over the valley and was gliding toward the mountaintops behind the village. The day was more than half over but the noises from the feast were growing louder. He thought he could even make out the sound of Mundo's flute.

"Hey, what's the matter?" said Ginevra, as Bart got up.

"Nothing's the matter," said Bart. "I just feel like going somewhere."

"Where?"

"Come on, I'll show you."

Bart led Ginevra to the weak part of the fence. "See this? If we push on it, we are small enough to get through. And then we can go visit places where the good plants grow. They're not far from here."

"I don't know. Mundo's not around and—"

"Exactly. He's busy enjoying himself with all the other villagers. He's not thinking about us. Anyway, we're not going far. We'll be back before he even shows up. And he told Peco not to leave the pasture. Come on, the plants up there are SWEET."

"Well . . . okay."

Bart's guess about the fence turned out to be correct and they pushed on it enough to create an opening they could wriggle through.

The two lambs jumped with excitement as they cut across the upper field. When they got to the dense brush line, they trotted along until a gap revealed a path heading upward. Sheep being good climbers, they soon were behind the hill in a glade they both remembered. They began searching for their favorite tasty plants.

Though the village was hidden from them, they could hear faintly the sounds of the villagers and a barking dog. *Peco must have noticed we're gone*, Bart thought. He didn't want Peco's barking to upset Ginevra and make her want to return right away.

"Let's go up higher just for a few minutes, and then we can go home," said Bart. He backtracked until he found a place where the trail branched off. Soon they reached a grassy hilltop surrounded by trees and dotted with a few large boulders.

Bart trotted right up to the edge of the knoll and Ginevra followed. "Whoa," she said. In front of them was a steep drop. The valley below looked something like the dale the Grange sat upon, only bigger. There was a large stone and brick building they could see in the distance. It had towers rising above the tallest trees.

The breeze up here was chilly, but Bart liked how it felt on his face. "Isn't this great?" he said.

"It sure is!" said Ginevra.

"I think Lord Giovanni lives in that castle over there," said Bart.

The sun was touching the top of the mountains, and Bart knew it would be getting dark in a short while. "We should go back now," he said to Ginevra. They turned around and made their way back through the little knoll. The shadows of the trees lying across the grassy area had lengthened.

They were nearly to the head of the trail when a trick of the eye, a hint of something wrong, made them halt in their tracks. There was a shadow within a shadow, and it was blocking their way.

Then the shadow moved. A shade-colored creature stared at them with yellow eyes. Though Bart had never seen one, his sheep instinct knew this ancient enemy instantly.

It was a wolf.

Chapter Five

The way the wolf stood stock still—the open space all around them—the cliff behind them—Ginevra's sudden trembling—the damp ground underneath his hooves—the low angle of the sunlight—the strange scent on the breeze. All these things Bart took in at once as time seemed to slow. He knew he had only a moment to act before Ginevra bolted and the wolf gave chase. He could not let her be seized by the wolf, or panic and run off the cliff. It was his fault she was in terrible danger, and she was his best friend.

The next instant his legs were pushing off the ground and his head was lowering. He charged right at the wolf, hoping to strike the animal's shoulder before its jaws had a chance to close around Bart's neck. He saw a surprised look on the wolf's face just before the beast dodged to the left.

Bart slammed to a stop, turned, and with his head still lowered, watched the wolf's movement. A dozen paces away, Ginevra was surprised by Bart's quick attack. A sheep's instinct was to run away from danger but also to stick close to the flock. She knew that if she ran from the wolf, she would be running away from Bart. She couldn't leave him. So as the wolf leapt onto a nearby boulder, she fought the urge to flee.

He's trying to get to the high ground to attack us easier, thought Bart, as he backed up to put himself between the wolf and Ginevra. He saw the wolf lowering himself to spring. *Here it comes*, thought Bart. The beast's snout wrinkled as it opened its mouth to reveal a long, red, dripping tongue, and terrible, pointed, white teeth.

Its mouth opened wider and wider and then . . .

Wait. Was it yawning?

"I beg your pardon," said the wolf, settling on all fours with a sigh and crossing his paws. "I didn't mean to frighten you. I was just curious about two lambs up in these hills all alone. And *attack* lambs, I might add. I've never run into that type before."

Bart was watching the beast closely, every muscle still tensed. He figured this was some kind of wolf trick.

"Now, now, I could very easily eat you, but I'm not going to," said the wolf.

"I don't believe you!" yelled Bart.

"But it's true," said the wolf. "I promised I would never attack any human's livestock—or any human for that matter. I intend to keep my promise. Let me introduce myself. I am known as the Wolf of Gubbio. But you may call me Lupo."

"I'm Bart, and this is Ginevra," said Bart, still ready for battle and trying to sound bigger and tougher than he felt. "We're from the village down below. Our shepherd is, uh, sure to come looking for us, uh, any moment now. He is very big and strong and carries a big staff and has a great big nasty dog."

The wolf chuckled. "I see. It's clear you haven't heard of me. I suppose I'll have to tell you my story to convince you I mean no harm. Just give me a second to get more comfortable. Old injury, you know," he said, shifting his weight and curling his tail around him.

Bart and Ginevra stood tensely still, watching the wolf's every move.

"So, here is my story: I was born far north of here in the high mountains. Like all wolves, I was taught by my pack, and I became a very good hunter. But we always stayed away from the towns where humans live. My pack got smaller over the years until it was just my mate and myself. And then one day my mate and our newborn cubs were killed in their den by men and dogs sent by the local lord. The men chased me and nearly killed me too. I just barely managed to escape and came south. For a while I lived in the wild, but I was alone, injured, and having trouble chasing down prey by myself.

"I hated and feared humans, but I was slowly starving. So I began to hang around this little mountain town. There I could snatch a chicken every once in a while. Sometimes even a kid goat or lamb. When people tried to stop me, I attacked them. But it was like stirring up a hive of bees. The townspeople started carrying clubs and going out in twos or threes. They brought their dogs with them and kept their livestock close by. I knew my easy hunting days were almost up.

"Then one day this man arrived in town with some of his Brothers. You may have heard of him. He is called Poverello, the Poor One."

Poverello! thought Bart with a jolt. *That must be the same man the lark and the hare talked about!*

"The townspeople must have told him about me," the wolf continued. "This man was not armed, yet he went looking for me. I was crouched down in the woods, but he saw me. He walked right up to me, and I snarled at him and prepared to attack. Then he stopped, held up his arm, and started to speak.

"'Peace and goodwill to you, Brother Wolf,' he said. I knew instantly he meant it. I could see this human didn't hate me, and I could smell he wasn't afraid, either. He said, 'It seems you have the whole town of Gubbio in an uproar because you have hurt their people and eaten their animals. Tell me why you are doing this? Why aren't you chasing deer far away from here?'

"I had never spoken to a human before. But somehow it seemed rude not to answer. I told him what had happened to my mate and about being chased by men and about my injuries. He listened quietly. When I was done, he was silent for a moment and then said, 'I understand now. And I am sorry for what has happened to you. You are one of God the Father's creatures and you have to eat. I have an idea, but you will have to promise me something.'

"I agreed to what he asked and together we walked toward the entrance of the town. I hung back behind the man, ready to flee. There were many people gathered and they looked, smelled, and sounded angry and fearful. But this poor man told them not to be afraid of me. He told them my story and said I had agreed to stop attacking them and their animals. Then he said, because I needed to eat in order to live, and I could no longer hunt wild game like deer, the townspeople should feed me.

"His words really got them buzzing. They didn't like the idea and I could tell by their smell they were all for killing me. But Poverello kept on telling them about God's love for them and for all his creatures. He also talked about forgiveness, which he said God believes in. Then a woman called out, and Poverello told me what she asked. 'The wolf is acting well with you, but how do we know he isn't still a wild beast who will tear us to pieces?'

"Poverello told her, 'He won't. He is quite tame now,' and then he turned to me and said, 'Come here, Brother Wolf.' I went and lay down on all fours next to him. 'Will you promise not to harm any people or their animals from now on?'

"'Yes,' I said, by lowering my head in a sign of respect. Then he held out his hand. I sat up, raised my paw and put it in his hand and he held it. All the people gasped and started making hand motions and murmuring. After he spoke to them a little longer, they began laughing and crying and hugging each other. Some of the young ones went running and quickly returned carrying pails. They brought them to where I sat and dumped them in front of me: stewed vegetables, bones, the bottom crusts from their porridge pots. It was a feast! I ate until I was totally full.

"Since then, the townspeople have kept an eye out for me. Every few days when I show up they bring me food. I have gotten to know a lot of them. They are now my friends. And I have kept my promise. I have never harmed a human or one of their animals since that day. That is why I am known as the Wolf of Gubbio. So, then—pleased to meet you, Bart and Ginevra."

By this time the two lambs had almost forgotten their fear, and they quickly remembered their manners. "Pleased to meet you, uh, Lupo, sir," Bart said.

"What are you doing here near our little settlement?" asked Ginevra.

Lupo shrugged. "Wolves like to roam. So does Poverello. A few days ago I heard him talking to the men he calls his Brothers about Christmas. He said it should be more than just a big feast and a time for giving lots of gifts. He wants it to be a very special day honoring God the Father's gift of love to the world—the gift of his only Son. So, he and some of these Brothers are coming to Greccio for the Christmas season. I thought I would follow him and see this Greccio for myself."

"Poverello came this way?" said Bart.

"Well, wolves can travel much farther than humans in a day. Even an old wolf like me. I got ahead of him. I expect he will be here sometime tomorrow . . ."

The wolf paused for a moment and perked his ears, then slowly got to his feet, wincing a bit. "And now I have to take my leave. That shepherd with his big dog you spoke about is on his way up here. I enjoyed meeting you. Please consider Lupo the Wolf of Gubbio your friend from now on." He turned and slipped into the woods, disappearing from sight in a few seconds.

"Goodbye, Mr. Lupo!" yelled Bart. There was no reply. Bart and Ginevra could hear rustling and growling coming from below them and getting closer. At first the sounds made the lambs nervous. But then they heard "Baaart! Gineeevra!" It was a voice they knew instantly, the voice of their shepherd. Soon Peco and then the boy reached the top of the knoll.

"There you are, you two rascals! Thank God! Come here. Are you all right?" said Mundo. He checked them over carefully for injuries.

"You gave me a real scare. Good thing Peco kept barking and whining until someone came and got me."

Peco, meanwhile, was ignoring them all. He was sniffing the boulder where the wolf had lain. The darker hairs on the ridge of his back rose and a growl rumbled loudly in his throat. Mundo got up and walked over to him.

"What is it, Peco boy?" He bent down and looked more closely at some mud on the rock that clearly showed the imprint of a large paw. As Mundo studied it, his mouth dropped open. He jerked his head around and gripped his staff tighter, but it was clear the beast was gone. He started searching around the boulder, looking closely at the soft ground. He stopped to examine some paw marks where the wolf dodged sideways. A little further on, he came upon the deep imprints where Bart dug in his hooves and charged. He let out a low whistle.

"This is incredible," he said. "Did you two run into a WOLF!?"

Bart proudly tossed his head, and Mundo started to laugh.

"And you survived! Such brave lambs! Bart, you are going to be a fine sheep when you grow up. Let's get you two home."

As they made their way past the boulder where the wolf had been lying, Mundo did a double take and moved closer to a thorn bush. He leaned over and carefully removed something from one of its branches, then tucked it into his pouch.

As they climbed down, the sun disappeared behind the mountains. Peco led the way and the lambs followed. Mundo brought up the rear. When they reached the part of the trail where dense brush cuts off the view of the steep slope behind and the pasture below, they were startled to hear a sharp *OW-AWOOO* coming from the mountainside. Mundo spun around, and Peco started barking furiously. The sound sent shivers down Bart's spine, but he and Ginevra weren't too alarmed. They knew it was just their new friend Lupo, the Wolf of Gubbio, saying goodbye.

Chapter Six

When they reached the gate to the common pasture, they were met by two of Mundo's cousins, Gino, who was a couple years younger than Mundo, and Tom, who was several years older. Tom had just gotten married to a girl from Greccio.

"There you are! You found them. We were starting to worry," Tom cried out.

"Yeah, especially after we heard that wolf howling," said Gino. "Or at least it sounded like a wolf."

"It was a wolf all right," said Mundo. "I'll tell you the whole story later. But first, did you block off that part of the fence we found broken? I don't want to take any chances of a lamb slipping out or a wolf slipping in until I can fix it tomorrow."

"All taken care of," said Tom.

"Thanks. I hope there's some food left."

"Always hungry, aren't you?" laughed Tom. "Don't worry, Aunt Lina saved you plenty. We'll tell Uncle Vin you found the lambs and you're okay. See you at the bonfire." And the two young men left.

"Now, you two," said Mundo to the lambs. "Into the pen with you."

Bart trotted right in, followed by Ginevra. Mundo latched the gate behind them. Then he reached down and took Peco's head in his hands.

"We found them, thanks to you, boy. Now you stay here and I'm going to bring you back the best meal you've had in a long time."

Mundo was as good as his word. Before long he returned with a slab of meat pie as big as his hand.

"You get my portion tonight, Peco. You deserve it." Peco lay down on all fours and when Mundo put the pie between his front paws the dog took time to sniff it all over, very gently and carefully. Then he gulped it down in three huge bites. He spent another minute licking up every last crumb.

Mundo went to his hut. When he emerged a few minutes later, his face looked cleaner, his brown curls were tied back with a piece of rawhide, and he had his shepherd's pipe in his hand.

By now, benches at the grange had been brought out for the older folk. A bonfire was roaring nearby, spitting sparks, like so many fireflies, into the air. The villagers gathered around it, drawn to its growing, dancing flames.

No sooner had the shepherd arrived than his uncle said in his booming voice, "Mundo, what's all this about a wolf?" The crowd quickly quieted and moved closer as Mundo started to tell his tale. He spoke slowly in a clear voice about Peco's barking and carrying on, which alerted him to the disappearance of the two lambs and then to the discovery of the broken fence.

"I started calling them. Then Peco caught a scent and began running up this hill," said Mundo, his eyes scanning the staring faces in front of him. "When we reached the top there were the two lambs. I was so relieved and went to check that they were okay. Peco, though, went straight to this big rock and started sniffing and growling deep in his throat and carrying on. It made my neck prickle just to hear him. I went over to him and there, in the mud, was a paw print as big as my hand. The print of a wolf."

"You are just trying to scare us, Mundo," said his aunt. But they were all listening, eyes wide.

"I thought I heard a wolf howling a little while ago," said one man.

"We heard it too, Gino and I," said Tom. "Right before Mundo got back."

That caused the villagers to exclaim and start a few arguments. Mundo took a step closer to the fire, as if he had more to say, and the chatter died down.

"Oh, it was a wolf all right," said Mundo. "I have proof." He paused, then slowly pulled something dark and fuzzy from his pocket. He held the tuft of wolf fur up in the firelight for all to see. Two young girls sitting close to him squealed. Mundo flashed a big grin, then he was all serious again. "We must have gotten there just in time to scare it away," he said. "Peco would have chased after him if I hadn't stopped him. Those lambs were brave, but of course *they* are no match for a wolf." He looked around at the faces as his words sunk in.

People glanced uneasily in the direction of the mountains. Outside the bonfire's circle of light there was nothing but blackness. Children shivered with fear and excitement. The older boys looked at Mundo with new respect in their eyes. Then, one gray-haired old man started telling a story about packs of wolves descending on mountain towns long ago. That got the youngsters even more worked up. Finally,

Mundo's Aunt Lina put her foot down. "That's it. No more talk of wolves! Let's have some music. Gino, you and the lads help get the grange floor ready so we can dance. Mundo, we're going to need that flute of yours."

The men, women, and children began to make their way over to the grange building. The older boys and girls removed the makeshift tables from the hard-packed dirt floor and lit torches set in holders on the stone walls. The tall, heavy wooden doors of the grange were opened to the night air and a view of the bonfire, which by now was throwing sparks and flames high into the air.

Stools were brought for Mundo and his friend Stefano, who played the drum. With a "one, two, three!" they began a lively tune. On one of the benches, a grandmother wrapped in layers of cloth against the night chill clapped her wrinkled hands.

"Dance! Dance!" she cried.

Several barefoot children ran to the middle of the hard dirt floor and began swinging each other around or hopping up and down to the beat of the music. By the second song, the grange floor was swarming with dancers young and old.

Then Mundo played the opening notes of a popular song called "The Fair Shepherdess." The villagers threw up a cry of delight, and hurried to join hands in double circles, the inside ones facing out and the outside ones facing in.

In a strong, clear, voice, Mundo sang:

Her laughter rings from high to low
A vision on a hill I see
Her eyes do shine, her cheeks do glow
She must a fairy maiden be

Now the two circles of dancers began to move, in opposite directions. Mundo put his flute to his lips and played the bouncy melody of the chorus and everyone sang:

The Shepherdess she leads her flock along her merry way
With lovely voice she calls to them oh hey my lambs oh hey
The bloom of youth adorns her brow, her steps so lightly
spring
Forever will I see her grace and of her charms will sing

The dancers fell silent and paused as Mundo sang another verse. Then they took up the chorus again as they circled in reverse. Mundo sang more verses, and each time he and Stefano played the chorus just a little bit faster. Soon the circles of dancers whirled by each other at dizzying speed, their smiling, breathless faces flashing by. Finally, the song ended in a rattle of the drum and a high flute blast. A great cheer went up and there were cries of "Bravo, Mundo! Bravo, Stefano!" The two boys beamed.

A youngster approached them with a waterbag and honey cakes in his hand. "Ah, the life of a musician," said Stefano. He took a honey cake from the boy and downed it in two bites, then licked the crumbs off his fingers. "Mundo—that was great, when did you learn to play like that? You should have seen the girls looking at you when you sang." Stefano struck the drum for emphasis. Mundo sipped from the waterbag while he caught his breath. His face shone with sweat and happiness.

"You weren't so bad yourself, Stefano," said Mundo, eating his own cake more slowly. "I hate to admit it, but I guess those hands of yours are good for something besides fixing broken wagon wheels." Like almost all the villagers,

Stefano worked in the fields, but he also had other jobs. He was very clever with any kind of wooden thing in need of repair. He made his own drum from wood and a stretched piece of animal skin, and was presently working on making a tambourine.

After a little while, the boys settled back on their bench and Mundo started playing another new tune he had been practicing all summer. The dirt dance floor was full in seconds. Mundo and Stefano looked at each other, flashed smiles and kept playing.

In the dark of their pen, the sheep and goats were listening closely to Bart and Ginevra describe what it was like meeting the Wolf of Gubbio.

"Weren't you terrified when that wolf appeared?" asked an older lamb.

"Sure, I can't lie, it was scary and I thought we were done for. But I wasn't going to die without a fight," said Bart, proudly.

"And I was going to stick with Bart until the end," said Ginevra, just as proudly.

When they were finished telling their story, Bart and Ginevra were peppered with a million more questions, until finally Nana goat piped up. "Okay, now, that's enough. We've all had plenty of excitement for one day. All I can say is next time you lambs might think twice about how dangerous it is to leave the safety of the flock. Just because you are brave and loyal doesn't mean you can't get eaten! Now, everyone, go to sleep!"

Bart had to smile when Nana called him brave and loyal. He settled himself down a little apart from the others, close to the gate of the pen. He wanted to be the first one up at dawn. Already he was making plans in his head. He fell asleep at last, remembering the look of surprise in the wolf's eyes when he charged at him, and Mundo saying, "You are going to be a fine sheep when you grow up."

Chapter Seven

The music and dancing went on for a long while. Each time Mundo and Stefano took a break, someone handed them something to eat. Mundo would take a few bites and shove the rest into his waist pouch. When it got late the older people started to say their goodnights first. They were followed by the little children and their parents, until only the youths were left. These older boys and girls moved back to the warmth of the bonfire, which was dying down to glowing embers. They all gathered around Mundo and Stefano, begging them to play certain songs. Then they sang along, or tried to make each other laugh, or just talked. Finally, Mundo's Uncle Vin walked over and announced St. Martin's Day was over. "Off to home and bed, the lot of you," he said. Mundo fell into his bed fully clothed, and was asleep nearly at once with a lingering smile on his face.

The next morning as the darkness began to thin out, none of the villagers stirred. But Bart was already awake, determined to keep an eye on the road every minute from sunrise on. He knew it would be hard to stand on his hind legs very long to see over the pen's walls. He really needed to be out in the pasture. This was just too important.

So he set to work on the metal loop holding the gate closed. Very quietly, so as not to wake anyone else, he nudged it up, up, up with his nose, and didn't give up every time it fell back. Finally, after many tries, he did it. The gate was unlatched. He shoved his nose between the gate and the post and pushed his way out of the pen. Then he pushed the gate closed behind him, so it would take the rest of the flock longer to realize it was open.

He trotted over to Jaco's and Violeta's stalls to tell them the rest of what the wolf said to him and Ginevra the day before about the kind, poor man known as Poverello. "He talked about God the Father, so God and his Father must be the same person," said Bart. "And remember the lark said the Poor One talked about his Father being the Creator. So God must be his Father *and* the Creator!"

"Hmmph" said Jaco.

"Lupo also said Poverello wants Christmas to be a day honoring the Father's gift of love to the world, and that gift was his only son."

He heard Violeta make that squeaky, breathy sound of hers. "What is it, Violeta?" Bart said.

"Oh, nothing, really. Your story just makes me think of my son Seymour. I hope wherever he is, he is warm and has enough to eat. Go on, Bart, dear."

"And then Lupo told us Poverello was on his way to Greccio, and he was going ahead of Poverello. That's when he heard Mundo and Peco coming up the trail and he got up and disappeared into the woods. He kept his word and never tried to harm us. He was ever so polite."

"Are you sure he was a wolf?" asked Jaco. "He sounds much too tame."

"Oh, he was a wolf all right. You should have seen those teeth," said Bart with a shudder. "The best part is . . . well, I guess the best part is he didn't eat us. But the next best part is Poverello should be passing by here sometime today. I just know he's the same man the hare and the lark were talking about. I don't want to miss seeing him. Actually, it's getting light now so I had better start watching."

He excused himself and trotted to the high part of the pasture. Bart peered toward the northern end of the road. As dawn broke it was becoming gradually more visible. He was looking for anyone who might be traveling south toward Greccio. Soon the village started to awaken. Bart could hear the sound of Mundo's flute coming from his hut. It was a song he played over and over the night before at the urging of the villagers. *A very happy tune*, Bart thought. *Soon the boy will be up and about.*

Sure enough, a few minutes later, Mundo came out of his hut, just in time to see the last of the sheep and goats escaping the pen and spilling into the pasture.

"I don't believe it. Not again!" cried Mundo. Then he looked around and spotted Bart clear at the other end of the pasture. "Bart, I know this is all your doing!" shouted Mundo.

He quickly threw some hay into Violeta's and Jaco's stalls so they would be well fed before their day's work began. Then he headed for the center of the village. In a little while he returned, with a hammer and a nail bent into the shape of a staple. He went right to the sheep pen and hammered both ends of the staple into the outside of the pen near the metal loop latch. Then he tied a rope to the loop and threaded it through the staple. Now the latch could be tied down from the outside, where a little lamb couldn't nibble it free.

"That ought to hold him," Mundo muttered when he finished.

He sat down on the old oak stump and took food out of his pouch he saved from the night before. There were pieces of sausages, fritter, and cake. He ate slowly, sighing over every bite. When he was done, he took his flute out of his pouch and played a little part of a song, over and over, until the melody flowed.

Bart grazed at the highest corner of the pasture, constantly raising his head to look at the road running south. He jumped in surprise when the grass near his hooves moved. Up popped a hare.

"Bart, it's me, Seconda," said the hare. "Remember those poor men I told you about? Well, they're coming!"

"Hello Seconda. Yes, that's who I'm hoping to see!"

Just then, in the distance, four men appeared on the road, walking two by two. They carried walking sticks made from branches.

"Seconda, there are four men walking this way wearing long robes the color of your fur. Could this be them?" asked Bart, studying them intently.

Seconda stood up on her hind legs and twitched her nose as she watched the men draw closer. Bart saw that their faces had short beards, and when one man lowered his head, Bart could see it was shaved on top. One man had the strong and heavy build of a knight, one was tall, one had a round little belly, and one was slight of build.

Bart could hear the faint murmur of the men talking to each other. As the road swung clear of the mountain wall, their voices suddenly joined and changed. They were singing. "That's them, that's them!" said Seconda.

Beside himself with excitement, Bart didn't want to just watch them pass by. He wanted to see and hear them – especially Poverello – up close. Maybe they would stop to get a drink. But what if they didn't? They only had a couple more miles to go before they reached the town of Greccio. How could he make sure they stopped here at the

Grange village? *Now* was when Bart had to do something, and quickly.

"Thank you Seconda, and goodbye!" said Bart.

He ran downhill as fast as he could, ears bouncing, straight through a knot of grazing sheep. "It's him, it's Poverello!" He shouted to them at the top of his lungs. "Start making noise, everyone! We've got to get their attention!"

"Poverello! Poverello!" he cried as he went running across the pasture toward the stable. Ginevra caught on right away and joined in.

"Poverello! Poverello!" she shouted. Then she began running and doing high springing jumps over the grass. That got the older lambs dashing about madly. The ewes started bleating loudly. The goats loved any reason to make a lot of noise.

"Puh-uh-uh verello!" they cried.

"Jaco, Violeta!!" cried Bart as he passed by the stable at a run, "That's him, that's Poverello!" Violeta's nostrils flared and she began her breathy *hee-haw*-ing. It was not very loud, but it helped.

The men on the road slowed and were staring in surprise, watching all the noisy animals running about. The potbellied one said loudly to the others, "Brothers, either they love our singing or this is how they've started greeting visitors to Greccio." The men chuckled at that.

Just then Jaco stamped the ground and bellowed "MOOOOverello!" loud enough to shake the last nuts from the trees in the orchard. The four men laughed even harder.

"That's it, everyone, keep it up," said Bart. "Poverello!" he shouted.

The Brother as big as a knight beamed at the slight man next to him. "They're happy to see you, Brother. It almost sounds like they're saying 'Poverello.'"

"Yes, Angelo," said the slight man with a smile. "It does sound like they're calling me." The group turned and walked the short way up the path toward the common pasture fence.

Bart saw the men coming and went running to the fence to meet them, followed by Ginevra and all the other sheep and goats. Violeta and Jaco stretched their necks way out of their stalls. Seeing Bart take off at a run and the whole flock going crazy, Mundo jumped up and made his way over as fast as he could. From the grange building and the cottages, from the fields below in the river valley, from every direction, villagers looked up at the commotion and hurried over to see what was going on.

As Mundo and the other Grangers got close, they slowed at the sight of the men's clothing and shaved heads. These were the men dedicated to God and known as the Poor Brothers. They were famous in these parts and were seen traveling this road before. The Poor Brothers lived on handouts like beggars. They owned very little beside the clothes on their backs. They helped the poor and the sick. Like their leader, they preached about the love of God to anyone who would listen. Their leader's fame reached far beyond Italy to all the Christian lands, but that had not changed him, people said.

Mundo walked through the loudly bleating sheep and goats, his quick eye looking them over. But he saw nothing amiss. As he reached the fence, he looked into the eyes of the man who stood closest to him and gave a little start.

"Peace and goodwill, young man. Peace and goodwill to you, sheep, and to you, goats, and to you, Lady Donkey, and you, Sir Ox," said the slight man.

At the sound of the man's voice, Bart and the other animals quieted instantly. Bart knew right away this indeed must be the same man the hare, the lark and the wolf told him about. He wasn't much to look at—thin and not very tall. His body looked old and worn down, but his face seemed young and lively when he spoke. Then there was his voice. It was as charming and inviting as a mountain breeze. Bart thought he could listen to it forever.

"I am Brother Francesco, and these are my companions, Brothers Giles, Angelo, and Simon."

"I know who you are, Brother Francesco. I'm Mundo, uh, welcome to our village."

"We are on our way to Greccio but couldn't help noticing these fine animals you have here," said the large one named Angelo. "They're so full of . . . joy."

"And God loves a joyful noise," said Brother Francesco.

"Yes, he *does!*" said the tall young Brother Simon, with a big smile. The other three chuckled as if he told a fine joke.

By this time it seemed like everyone in the village was running over and gathering behind Mundo. Some of the men still had tools in their hands. "It's Brother Francesco, the Poverello," they whispered urgently to one another. Mundo turned his head and saw people moving their hands across their heads and chests in the sign of the cross and bowing or curtsying toward the men in a sign of respect. Mundo blushed, and looked down. He hadn't crossed himself or bowed. But Brother Francesco didn't seem to notice or care.

He looked right at Mundo, and his narrow face lifted in a smile to match his merry eyes. "Are these delightful animals under your care, Mundo?"

"Yes, sir, uh, Brother Francesco," said Mundo.

"So, you are their shepherd. Are they always this friendly?" he asked. He looked at the flock in front of him wagging their tails and the ox and donkey in their stalls with their necks stretched out. Every animal was staring at Francesco as if he was about to give them all a delicious treat.

"Yes. Uh, no. Well, actually, I've never seen them like this. I don't know what's gotten into them."

Two children who were sent to the well to fetch water came running up, breathless, with a bucket and a ladle. They offered it to Francesco and his friends. The Brothers thanked them, leaned their walking sticks against the fence, and drank in turn.

Then Francesco spoke, looking at Mundo and all those standing behind him. "Thank you all for your kindness," he said, raising his voice to reach the growing little crowd. "We are on our way to see Lord Giovanni. As you may know, he has given our brotherhood a little piece of the mountain as a quiet place for us to live and spend time praying. This is the Christmas season though, and we are planning something special for everyone in these parts. It will take place on Christmas Eve. It's something I've wanted to do for a long time. Something never been done before outside the Holy Land. Something that will help us honor the great gift of love God our Father and Creator gave us." Brother Francesco's eyes sparkled.

"Instead of staying indoors and playing games and passing out gifts, we'd like people to really imagine that wonderful night when Baby Jesus was born. How amazing that was! Did you know the Christ child was born to a poor family in a village much like this one? With beasts like these for company?" He waved his arm in the direction of Jaco and Violeta.

Brother Francesco paused and seemed to be thinking a moment. Everyone held their breath and waited. Then he raised his chin toward Jaco and Violeta and spoke directly to them.

"Sir Ox, Lady Donkey, I have a favor to ask of you. Would you agree to give up some of your rest and help us on Christmas Eve?"

Violeta *hee-hawed* gently and Jaco gave a low *moo*. The villagers chattered in surprise. Brother Francesco just smiled.

He turned back to the people. "They have agreed to help, so now it's up to their village and their shepherd. Mundo, can you and the village lend us the services of your donkey and your ox on Christmas Eve? They would not have to do any hard work and they would be fed and cared for."

Mundo looked around for his uncle, who had just joined the group, and caught his eye. His uncle spoke right up.

"Of course, Brother Francesco, anything the Poor Brothers want. It would be an honor."

"Good. Then would you, Mundo, bring them to Greccio at midday on Christmas Eve?"

"Yes, Brother Francesco," said Mundo, still wearing a startled look.

"We could use a shepherd too. Can you wear your shepherd's cloak and bring your shepherd's staff? And I notice you have a flute."

Mundo looked at the flute in his hand as if surprised he was still holding it.

"Do you know the songs . . ." and Francesco named some well-known tunes. Mundo nodded and said yes, he could play them.

"Well, that will be a big help," said Brother Francesco. "Your talents are just what we need to help give glory to God at Christmas."

At that moment Bart got up on his hind legs and leaned on the fence with his nose high in the air, hoping to get even closer to Brother Francesco.

"You would like to be a part of this too, eh little lamb?" said Francesco, looking down at him. Bart *baah-ed* loudly in agreement and wagged his tail. "Well, if your shepherd decides to bring you, that will be fine."

The Brother who looked like a jolly old peasant watched Francesco closely as he talked. Then he spoke up. "Aye, this village reminds me of the one I grew up in. Sturdy people and animals too. Brother, now that things are settled, we should leave these good folks to their work. I, for one, am looking forward to reaching Greccio and resting."

"Yes, Brother Giles. You're right," said Francesco, and for just a moment a weary look passed over his face. Then it was gone and he was smiling again.

"We must leave you now and finish our journey," he said. Just then, Aunt Lina came pushing through the knot of people, with something that looked like her almond cakes wrapped in a scrap of cloth. She pressed the bundle on tall young Brother Simon, who thanked her with a bow and a smile.

"May God bless you and keep you and make his face to shine upon you," said Francesco. "We hope to see you all the night of Christmas Eve. Take the high road to Greccio and look for the path to the caves on the right. You know the ones I mean—they are before you reach the town."

The four Brothers took up their walking sticks. Brother Angelo placed himself next to Francesco, who put his hand on the big man's arm and leaned on him slightly as they walked down the path to the road. There they turned and waved, and the villagers waved back. As they continued on their way, the breeze carried the sound of their voices singing in harmony:

All creatures of our God and King
Lift up your voice and with us sing

O praise him, Alleluia

Thou burning sun with golden beam
Thou silver moon with softer gleam

O praise him, O praise him
Alleluia, Alleluia, Alleluia!

Mundo and the villagers talked excitedly. Finally, everyone went back to work, and Mundo headed to the high pasture to repair the fence where Bart and Ginevra made their escape. It wasn't long before Bart came trotting up to watch Mundo work. The boy seemed a bit dazed.

"I can't believe it, Bart. Francesco himself, I got to meet him! Even better, he wants me to help him!"

Bart stood there and listened.

"I've heard stories about him my whole life," Mundo continued. "Did you know he's from Assisi, a town only four days travel from here? Once Grandfather and I walked half a day just to hear him preach in Terni. There were so many people there, spilling out of the church and filling up the square. I couldn't see him very well, so Grandfather put me on his shoulders. He spoke about the kingdom of God, and he pleaded with everyone not to turn their backs on

God's love. And there were rich lords there, and peasants and merchants and tradesmen, women and children, even beggars, all listening to him. By the time he was through people all around me were crying out to God, and tears were streaming down their faces. It scared me a little. I didn't know if they were crying from sorrow or from happiness. But I'll never forget it.

"And now this. A special celebration for Christmas Eve! And *I'm* going to be a part of it. I can't wait, Bart, I can't wait!"

Bart came over to Mundo and poked the boy's hand with his nose. Mundo reached over and scratched his back. Bart was happy for Mundo. But he was also worried. He wanted to be part of this special Christmas Eve too. Would Mundo take him with him?

Chapter Eight

As the days got chilly, it seemed like the sun was in more of a hurry to cross the sky and settle down in its cozy bed behind the mountains. Mundo took the sheep and goats foraging each day so they didn't over-graze the common pasture. They went up into the foothills of the mountains, or as far as the river's edge looking for grass, crop stubble, weeds—anything still green that would fill their stomachs before the short day turned to night.

The women of the little settlement were busy pickling vegetables, drying fruit, and mending winter clothes, when they weren't cooking or cleaning. The children added rotted manure to the gardens by the basketful, between lugging water and wood, fetching tools, babysitting the littlest ones, carrying bread from the village oven, and helping their parents any way they could.

Some of the men, led by Mundo's uncle, were digging trenches in the fields down by the river to keep them from being too flooded come springtime. Others were repairing the thatched cottage roofs, digging new waste pits for the outhouses, repairing tools, pruning olive, fruit and nut trees, and stacking wood. Bart was mostly away all day with the flock and inside the pen all night. But he did catch sight of Violeta a few times loaded down with straw thatch or wood or soil. She could carry so much more than a person could.

One day Mundo let the flock stay in the common pasture while he helped his cousin Tom, who was collecting materials to build a one-room cottage for himself and his new wife. With Jaco's help, Tom and Mundo were able to drag some heavy cornerstones into place to start the foundation.

As the light began to fade, the men returned from digging trenches and led a muddy Violeta back to her stall. Bart trotted over to speak with her while she waited for Mundo to arrive with Jaco.

"Good evening, Violeta," said Bart. "Can you tell me how long until Christmas Eve? It seems like it should be here by now."

"It won't be long. I'm sure looking forward to those twelve days of mostly resting. Gee, there's been a lot of work this fall! It's a good thing because it means the crops were plentiful. There wasn't a drought or too much flooding. Jaco's been hauling carts of grain down to the mill to be ground into flour about every other day. Much of it will be going to Lord Giovanni, of course, but the villagers have more than enough to last them the winter. Have you seen anyone cutting holly branches yet?"

"If you mean that shrub with the dark green prickly leaves and the red berries? Yes, I did see some children with a basketful of cut branches."

"Well, then, that's a sure sign Christmas Eve is just a few days away."

"There's something else I wanted to ask you," said Bart. "I've been thinking about what Poverello, uh, Brother Francesco, has been telling creatures about belonging to God the Creator. What do you know about these things called love, honor, and praise?"

"Hmm," said Violeta. "Love is easy to understand. I love my son Seymour, for instance. Just like your mother loved you."

Bart hung his head. "I don't remember her."

"Listen to me, Bart," said Violeta. "You may have been with her for only a few days, but in that short time she took care of you, fed you, protected you. She taught you things and helped you. She knew your heart. She loved you."

"Is that the way you feel about Seymour?" asked Bart.

"Yes, it is," said Violeta. "My Seymour is clever, like you, Bart. He is friendly and curious and loves to play. Mundo's grandfather was training him, and he was learning quickly and was very willing to work hard. Already he was used to carrying things on his back. But since he was not yet two, they didn't make him carry heavy things. I'm sure he is much bigger and stronger by now.

"It's been many seasons since he's been gone. I remember that awful day. If only I hadn't brayed so loudly when those men came! They made me so nervous with their loud voices and shiny weapons and their horses pawing and stamping the ground. Had I kept quiet maybe they would have left without coming over to our stall and seeing Seymour and taking him."

"It wasn't your fault, Violeta," said Bart. "You said Lord Giovanni gets most of the crops and the animals the villagers raise anyway, so maybe he just wanted a fine young donkey to help carry wood and hay."

Violeta sighed. "I know Seymour was old enough he didn't need to be with his mother anymore. It's not that. I just wish I knew he's alive and has a good master, who doesn't beat him or let him get sores on his back. It's not knowing that's so hard. I think of him every day. I just hope he has a good life."

"So . . . wanting good things for someone and thinking about them a lot and missing them, that's love?" asked Bart.

"That's part of it, for sure," said Violeta. "And Bart, even though your mother is gone, there are others here who love you, you must know that."

Bart was quiet for a moment thinking about that.

"What about praise?" he asked.

"That's easy," said Violeta. "If I tell you something wonderful about who you are or what you've done, that's praise."

"Hmm," said Bart. "Then that just leaves honor. How do you honor someone?"

"I'm afraid I don't know the answer to that, Bart. I've never heard of that before. But that man Brother Francesco said he was planning to honor God the Creator on Christmas Eve, and Jaco and I agreed to be part of it. I will try to figure it out when the time comes, and let you know."

Just then Mundo came trudging up to the stalls, leading Jaco. He put Jaco in his stall, then turned to the donkey.

"Hey there, Violeta girl. Hanging out with your buddy Bart, I see. Oh boy look at you. They've gone and gotten you pretty muddy," said Mundo. He reached into a bin for a piece of burlap sacking then went into the stall and started rubbing the mud off Violeta's legs.

"Only two days until Christmas Eve!" Mundo exclaimed, suddenly. Bart was all ears when he heard this. "You know I just got a message that the Brothers want me to come tomorrow to practice for the Christmas Eve celebration. I have to walk up to their hermitage—that's a place hidden away from everyone so the Brothers can live by themselves and spend a lot of time praying. I'll be back the next morning, Violeta, to get you and Jaco all groomed and ready. We'll head up to Greccio at midday."

Then he looked at Bart. "Cousin Gino will be taking care of the flock tomorrow while I'm gone. With Peco's help, of course. I've told him to let you all graze between the pasture and the road. That way he only has to keep an eye on the area between the fence and the stone wall. Bart, I need you to help keep everyone together. No taking off on your own or getting everybody all worked up while I'm gone. You have to behave."

Bart tossed his head in agreement. But Mundo still hadn't said he was planning to take Bart with him Christmas Eve, and that was what mattered most right now. If he had to act like the perfect lamb for the next two days, he would do it. Even if he knew deep down he was nothing like a perfect lamb. He hoped it was going to be enough to convince Mundo he deserved to go.

While he was still standing there, Ginevra came up to him.

"Hey, Bart, what's up?" she asked.

"I just heard Mundo say Christmas Eve is the day after tomorrow."

"That's great. Maybe you'll get to go."

"That's just it," Bart replied nervously. "He didn't say anything about me going. And I really want to."

"Well, even if you don't, I'm sure Violeta and Jaco will tell you all about it," said Ginevra.

"Yes, I know that. I just have a feeling this Christmas Eve celebration Poverello is planning is important—it will help me answer all the questions I've had lately. I'd really like to be there myself."

"I believe you will be," said Ginevra. "But that's two days away. No use wondering about something that hasn't happened yet. I have a better idea. I wonder. . . can I still jump higher than you? Catch me if you can!" And with that Ginevra took off across the pasture.

Bart only paused for a second and then chased after her. She headed for the stump and he was right behind her as she launched high into the air and threw in a half twist for good measure. He kicked upward and cleared the stump easily. Together they raced across the pasture. "The pile!" Ginevra shouted.

She leaned into a turn and headed for the manure pile near the stalls. It grew taller all year long until it was as tall as the stable. Recently, village kids started carting it away for their family gardens, which shrunk its size quite a bit. But Bart could see it was still nearly as high as Violeta's back and more than twice as wide. He had never jumped over something so big.

"Let's do it!" she cried and pumped her legs. Just as it seemed she would crash into the pile she pushed off, tucking her hind legs beneath her. "*Whaaaaa!*" Ginevra cried out as she made her leap. Bart was right behind her, the pile towering over him. But at the last second he swung to the right and jumped over the edge where it was not nearly so high.

"That was really fun!" huffed Ginevra.

"Yeah! You were amazing," said Bart breathlessly.

"You should have jumped the middle too! You can't chicken out—just decide to go for it. I know you can do it," said Ginevra.

"You really think so?" said Bart. "Gee, thanks, Ginevra."

They walked back side by side past the stables. Bart could see Mundo was finished rubbing down and checking Violeta, and was already working on Jaco. Very shortly he would feed them both some hay, then he would come for the flock. Bart trotted toward the pen to be at its gate well before Mundo arrived. He knew once he went there, the other goats and lambs would notice, stop their grazing, and come join him one by one. Then Mundo would not need to round them all up. As he waited, the words of the lark kept coming back to him. *Maybe you can find another way to give praise and honor to the one who made you, little lamb.*

Chapter Nine

Two days later, in the darkness just before sunrise on the morning of Christmas Eve, Bart felt cold winds blow. Rain started to fall. But soon something began to happen to the rain. It hissed as it fell and stung a bit when it hit his ears. A few minutes later the sound of the wind died away. The *hiss* of the stinging rain softened to a *hush* that seemed to muffle all other sounds. Something very soft and cold and light was falling out of the air onto his nose, head and back. Bart lay very still. He felt like he was the only one alive in this strange new world. He heard nothing except the faint *hush*, and saw nothing beyond the grayness.

He closed his eyes and must have dozed off, because when he opened them again the grayness was gone and the sun was gleaming under clouds bunched up on the horizon. He got to his feet, instantly aware this was the day he'd been waiting for. Then he noticed things around him were coated with fluffy whiteness. It lay on sheep's backs and goat's horns, on the top of fence posts. And when he got up on his hind legs to look over the pen's walls, the whole world seemed dusted in white. It was peaceful and incredibly beautiful.

"What's the matter, never seen snow before?" said Nana goat in his ear, chuckling at her own joke. *So this is snow,* thought Bart. *Violeta said it could come about Christmastime.*

"Well, get your fill of it. Won't last long. Going to get warm once the sun comes out," Nana added.

Pretty soon the boy Gino, wearing a cloak and a woolen cap down over his ears, arrived to let the flock out of the pen into the pasture. The lambs and kids went dashing through the rapidly disappearing snow. Bart heard children in the village running about and yelling to each other and doing their best to collect the thin layer of wet cold stuff in baskets before it all melted.

Bart trotted over to the part of the pasture where he could best watch the road coming north from Greccio. About mid-morning he saw Mundo—for he was the only one it could be who had that certain way of walking—coming around the bend.

The boy went right to the stable and fed Violeta and Jaco some hay, then began grooming them as they ate, picking the pebbles and mud and grass out of their hoofs, rubbing dirt off their backs and stomachs with a rag and then brushing them all over until their coats gleamed. Bart came over and stood near the stable in full view so Mundo wouldn't have to go looking for him. As Mundo was finishing up, his aunt and Gino came walking up.

"Are you leaving already, Mundo?" his aunt asked.

"Yes, soon. I want to get there with plenty of time, then I can rest. And the animals can be nice and settled in for tonight. The Brothers will feed me supper, Aunt Lina."

"Well, don't be surprised if most of the village shows up tonight. We'll bring lanterns and plan to arrive at the turnoff to the caves by three hours after sundown, like you said. We will wait there. And now here is your Christmas present from me. It's early, but I thought you could use it. Merry Christmas!"

She handed him something soft, tied with colored string. Mundo undid the string and held up a pair of leg-shaped woolen hose with a drawstring waist.

"Oh, Aunt Lina, thank you! My old hose has so many holes and patches and these are really nice and they look warm. I shall take good care of them and only wear them on special occasions—uh, well, like tonight!"

"I know you can't tell me about tonight because it's a surprise, but I want you to know we are all proud of you," she said, then hugged Mundo and left.

"I'll go and get the gate for you, Mundo," said Gino. "See you tonight."

By this time, Bart was really worried. Mundo had not even looked in his direction. He started pacing back and forth. Mundo ducked back into his hut and emerged with a bundle on his back, and some ropes and halters in the other. He put ropes and halters on Jaco and Violeta, then tied the donkey behind the ox. He stood there fiddling with another rope as Bart danced around in nervous circles.

"Okay, Bart. Brother Francesco says the shepherd can have a sheep with him too, so come here."

With his heart pounding, Bart trotted up to Mundo and let him put the rope halter around his head. Mundo tied the other end to Violeta.

"Anyway, if I bring you, I don't have to wonder what you are up to while I'm gone. Now you *must* behave and stay where I put you. This is going to be a very special night. Can you do that?"

Bart tossed his head in agreement.

"I'll take that as a yes," said Mundo.

Ginevra came running up. "Oh, Bart, you see, you *are* going! I knew Mundo would take you."

"I can hardly believe it!" said Bart. "I get to see what Christmas is all about! I promise to remember everything and tell you when we get back."

Mundo led the animals through the pasture gate and down the path from the village. A thin layer of mud and melting snow covered the road. The sun was chasing away the remaining clouds. Looking across the valley below them, Bart saw hoods of white now capped the highest mountains. Before he knew it, they walked around the edge of the mountain's knee and were headed along the back side of it.

The road was not very steep at first and they passed brown and white fields, bare vineyards and gray-leaved olive trees looking even more silvery with their dusting of snow. As the road rose, fields turned into woods. Bart saw familiar trees: sturdy oaks, beeches with their smooth bark, and the crooked shapes of hornbeams. A few grazing goats could be spotted here and there. After about an hour, they reached a fork in the road. "If we kept going we would reach the town of Greccio," said Mundo, "but we are going to turn off here. We're almost there."

Mundo and the little parade of animals climbed a steep and curving foot trail toward a rocky mountain wall. Near the wall the path narrowed then turned and widened out onto a broad ledge. They passed a row of shelters built out of tree limbs with roofs made of leaves. None was even as big as Mundo's hut. They almost seemed to grow right out of the rock wall.

Bart slowed to stare, wondering what kind of creature made them. But Mundo turned and called him. "Come on, Bart. That's just where the Brothers sleep," he said.

Mundo stared at a young man walking toward them. He was dressed in a short tunic and a sheepskin shepherd's cloak.

Mundo smiled. "Hello, Brother Simon, I hardly recognized you!"

"Peace to you, Mundo, my friend," said Simon, loudly. "I'm ready to be your fellow shepherd this night. I am greatly honored."

"Really?" said Mundo, grinning. "So how did you get chosen for this great honor?"

"Well, uh, as you know I have a voice that carries far and . . ."

"And what?"

"And, well, they don't really, uh, need me to sing. I do have a strong singing voice. But, alas, I have a tin ear. I'm never in tune."

Mundo grinned wider, then both of them laughed.

"So, Brother shepherd," said Simon, "let me show you where you can put the animals for the time being."

Simon led them to the end of the trail where some small trees grew against large fallen boulders. There Mundo tied each animal to a separate tree apart from one another and fetched them pails of water. Simon dropped an armload of hay in front of the ox and then the donkey. Bart started nibbling on a few stray weeds poking out from under a rock. It wasn't much, but Bart was used to making the best of things by eating whatever was at hand.

"Merry Christmas, Bart!" said Mundo as he walked up to the sheep with big handfuls of hay. "Eat up!" Bart couldn't believe his eyes. All this delicious hay, just for him? He dove right in.

He ate every bit then settled down to chew his cud. Violeta and Jaco, who ate much slower, were still working on theirs. From this high point above the valley, Bart could see the stone towers of the castle at Greccio poking above the trees. Somewhere in the distance a church bell rang. To his left, if he peered through the tree branches, he could see the entire Rieti Valley stretching for miles and miles, ending in hazy gray and white mountains.

The flock of Brothers moved about as busy as bees and as excited as children. Bart kept a lookout for Mundo but the boy was nowhere to be seen. Bart thought he heard his flute, though. Suddenly, in the afternoon, all the hubbub died down. When Bart looked around, he saw the last of the Brothers rush into a large shelter with a wooden cross on top. For a while, all was quiet but for some brief sounds of voices and singing. Then the men in their brown-gray robes came out and the hubbub began again. They all went back to work, carrying supplies, and setting things in place.

Bart even saw a few men come and go who wore tunics that had the outline of a castle with six towers sewn on them. "Violeta," he called out. "Who are those men working with the Brothers?"

"I've seen tunics like that before," she replied. "They must work for Lord Giovanni."

By the time the sun set, the clouds were gone and so was the breeze. The warmth of the afternoon was slowly fading. The last bit of rosy light disappeared behind the distant mountains. Stars began to shimmer overhead.

"Beautiful night isn't it?" said a low, familiar voice.

It took Bart a moment to spot the Wolf of Gubbio, whose gray fur blended into the dark, rocky landscape. It was only his yellow eyes that gave him away.

"Yes, it is, Lupo sir. Are you part of the celebration, too?"

"Let's just say I'll be watching and listening, but out of sight so I don't scare anyone. What about you? First an attack lamb, now a Christmas lamb," said Lupo with a chuckle.

"Thanks to you and my friend Seconda I met Poverello. I'm hoping this Christmas Eve will help me understand love, belonging, and, well, important stuff," said Bart.

"I'm sure if you listen with your heart, you will, my friend. Merry Christmas!" said Lupo. Then he slipped away into the darkness. Mundo came and gave Jaco and Violeta one more brushing. "Come on now, you two. It's time to get you into your spots for tonight's event." He led them away, and when he returned, Simon was with him, carrying a shepherd's crook and a lantern.

"I've found just the place to wait," said Simon to Mundo. "We will be where everyone can see us. Remember, no talking to anyone. From this moment on we are shepherds who have been tending our flocks in the fields by night."

Mundo untied Bart, and the lamb followed the two men down a steep shortcut to the mountain path. As they got near the main road, Bart could hear lots of voices below them. At the final curve, Simon had them cut through some brush. They stepped out onto a rocky ledge above the main road.

Then he turned to Mundo and said, in a booming voice, "Brother shepherd."

The people on the road below quieted down to listen.

"Let's rest here a moment, for we are almost there."

They sat on a rock, in plain view of the crowd. Already there were more people gathered than in the whole settlement of Greccio Grange. Others were arriving every minute, each little group led by someone carrying a lantern.

Bart saw everyone was bundled against the cold—some in fine robes richly dyed in deep colors, some in plain gray or brown homespun cloaks, some in clothes that were nearly rags. A few in front wore the long, coarse robes of Poor Brothers. There were old people, there were children, and most were somewhere in between. Everyone was on foot. They all talked excitedly. New arrivals were greeted with a hearty "Merry Christmas!" Bart saw Mundo's aunt and uncle arrive leading most of the villagers of Greccio Grange.

"There he is, there's Mundo and the sheep!" said Aunt Lina, loudly, pointing up at the rock where Bart sat. "Look, he's with another shepherd. Where is he from?"

"I don't know," said her husband. "Has Mundo told you what is going to happen?"

"No, of course not."

The number of arrivals kept growing, and the hubbub of voices grew louder. All of a sudden, candles started sparking to life in the hands of the Poor Brothers. The bubbling noise of the crowd drained away. Mothers and fathers lit candles for their children. Neighbors lit candles for each other. Some of the men and women wearing fine robes gave candles to those who had none.

Simon got to his feet.

"Come now," he said to Mundo in his loud voice. "We are on the edge of Bethlehem. It is not much farther. Let us go see this thing the angels told us about." Mundo stood.

The two shepherds, followed closely by the lamb, started to climb the path toward the mountainside.

The Poor Brothers in front of the crowd began to hum a tune in their throats. They motioned the people to join with them in singing. It was an ancient hymn that went like this:

> *O that birth forever blessed,*
> *When the virgin, full of grace,*
> *By the Holy Ghost conceiving,*
> *Bore the Savior of our race,*

The Brothers turned and walked as a group up the mountainside trail, trailing the shepherds. The crowd of townspeople followed eagerly, singing the familiar song.

> *And the Babe, the world's Redeemer,*
> *First revealed His sacred face,*
> *Forever more, forever more!*

As Bart walked around a curve and looked back, he saw what looked like a large swarm of fireflies, bobbing and floating up the hill behind them. Above him lights flashed through the trees, but it was impossible to make out what was up there.

They neared the side of the mountain where the path grew very narrow. Firepots placed at the edge of the trail gave off enough light to guide them. Then the way grew wide again and they passed the row of shelters along the rock wall. Each one was lit with a candle in a window or doorway, making them look like an inviting little village in some far-off land.

Farther up the mountain wall, something glowed brightly. But what was it? The townspeople gasped in astonishment and delight as they drew near enough to make out what it was.

There, above the mountain path, was a shallow cave, just wide enough for its purpose. Inside was a stable. An ox and a donkey stood there calmly, looking out over a low wall of rocks and tree branches. The cave was so brightly lit by torches and candles that every detail could be seen clearly. In front of the ox's and donkey's stalls, a young maiden, no more than seventeen, sat on a pile of straw. She was dressed in a homespun tunic. A long blue veil wrapped around her lovely face and reached down to her waist. A young man, also dressed in simple clothing, stood behind her with his hand on her shoulder. They gazed down at the cave's straw-covered floor. There, against a large rock, was an open wood box sitting on low, crossed wooden legs. It was a manger, a feed box used to give animals grain or hay or stubble to eat. But this one was filled with straw and held a little baby. He was all bundled in strips of cloth like a butterfly's cocoon. Only his face was showing. He was asleep.

The Poor Brothers beckoned the crowd forward. The people of Greccio crept up softly to the cave, as if expecting this wonderful vision to vanish at any moment. The shepherds and the lamb kept going and climbed onto a raised ledge just beyond the cave. Here they could be seen by everyone and still see into the cave as well.

Let no tongue on earth be silent,
Every voice in concert sing,
Forever more, forever more!

The song ended just as the last of the townspeople arrived. The crowd was now many times the size of Bart's little flock back home. Points of light disappeared as people blew out their candles. The shepherds and the Brothers knelt. With a rustling sound and whispers, the townspeople did the same.

Chapter Ten

Bart had never seen so many people gathered before. Why did they seem so excited? It was all really beautiful, of course, but what did it mean?

One of the Brothers walked forward. Bart noticed he was wearing a cloak with fine stitching on it. He began to speak to the people and at times they answered him, all together with one voice. Bart saw the people get to their feet, then kneel again, and then rise once more.

But his breath caught in his throat when a slight man with shining eyes stepped out of the line of Brothers and turned to face the crowd. Poverello!

Brother Francesco had a large book in his hands and he began to read aloud. Bart was amazed. It seemed like he was speaking in the language of sheep. And this was what it sounded like to Bart:

"There was a ruler named Caesar, and he commanded all the people to go to their home pasture to be counted. Joseph had to go to Bethlehem, because he was from the flock of David. He went with Mary, who was pledged to become his life-long mate. Mary was pregnant. While they were in Bethlehem, it came time for Mary to give birth, and she did, to a male child, her first son. There was no space left for them in the inn where the people were, so she had to give birth in a stable. She wrapped her baby in cloths and laid him in the box where animals are fed.

"That night, some shepherds were in fields nearby watching over their sheep. An angel—a great servant and messenger of God—appeared before them and the glory of God shone around them like the sun. The angel told the shepherds, 'Don't be afraid, I am bringing you good news that will be a joy to all people. Today the one who will save you was born in the town of David. He is Christ, the Lord. This is how you will know him: you will find a baby wrapped in cloths and lying in a feeding box.'

"So the shepherds went quickly and found Mary and Joseph and saw the baby lying in the feeding box. Then they told what the angels said about the child. Everyone was amazed when they heard what the shepherds said. Mary hid these things in her heart and kept thinking about them. Then the shepherds went back to their sheep, praising God and thanking him for everything they saw and heard. It was just as the angel told them."

Bart liked this story so much, he *baa-aa*-ed loudly when Francesco finished his reading. Francesco closed the book, kissed it, and handed it to one of the Brothers. Then he said, "And now the Brothers have a new song we want everyone to sing on this happy evening."

A note from Mundo's flute startled Bart. It hung in the air for many seconds, fluttered, then dove into a sweet melody. When it began to repeat, the Brothers sang the words to their new song. The third time around some people began to join in and by the fourth time everyone was singing along:

In Bethlehem is born the Holy Child,
On hay and straw in the winter wild,
O, our joy shall fill the earth
At Jesus' birth.

When it ended, Bart saw Francesco was standing in the torchlit stable between Jaco and Violeta. He raised his arms and began to speak:

"This night that we celebrate, twelve centuries after it happened, was a night like no other. We think of Christmastime and we think of feasting on good food, playing games, decorating our homes, and giving presents. But the Bible says God so loved the world he gave his one-of-a-kind and only Son. Let's stop and think about how God brought his beloved Son into the world. This Son Jesus, our Lord, is the King of kings, but were his earthly parents rich and powerful? No, his mother was a poor maiden, and his stepfather was a carpenter. Was he born in a castle? No. A manor? No. Was he born in a house? No. He was not even born in an inn. There was no room at the inn. He was born in a stable, with farm animals for company. An ox, a donkey. Their breath and the heat from their bodies is what kept him warm. He lay on straw like they did.

"And who were the first to hear from the angels about Jesus's birth? Shepherds, tending to their flocks at night.

Glorious angels brought the news about the birth of our Good Shepherd. And they brought it to humble peasants, those who care for sheep and lambs."

Bart was listening closely, and until now he was silent. But when he heard Francesco speak about the Good Shepherd, he opened his mouth and bleated as loudly as he could.

"Now what does the word 'humble' mean?" asked Francesco. "It means low in rank; it means willing to obey and serve others. It means not proud. It means meek. And what is more humble than beasts like oxen, donkeys and sheep? We think of such animals as things we own that serve us. They help feed us, clothe us, earn money for us. They are all around us, but we hardly notice them. When God chose for his Son to be born as a helpless babe among humble animals, what was he trying to tell us? Was it that we need to try and be higher and prouder and mightier than everyone else! No! Just the opposite!"

Baaa! cried Bart, as Francesco paused in his speech.

"Jesus told us, 'Blessed are the meek, the humble.' Our Lord taught us we should swallow our pride and admit we have sinned. We should turn away from our sins. Obey God's will. Think of others before we think of ourselves. Be meek and humble and follow him."

Francesco gazed tenderly down at the sleeping babe at his feet. The boy child was just beginning to stir. As he awoke and saw Francesco looking down at him, his eyes grew wide and he smiled. Francesco took a deep breath, and tears came to his eyes. Tears came to the eyes of many watching as well.

"The way to heaven," said Francesco in a low voice, "was opened wide by the Babe of Bethlehem, born to a poor virgin, among lowly animals. The Babe of Bethlehem, so meek and mild, who would be called the Lamb of God, who takes away the sins of the world. The Babe of Bethlehem, who came to earth to love us and save us and give us life everlasting. It is the very greatest Christmas gift we ever could, and ever will, receive."

With that, Francesco leaned over the manger and kissed the tiny babe on the forehead. For many long seconds, it seemed to Bart all sound disappeared from that mountainside in Greccio. Only light remained—from the torches and candles, from the stars overhead. Then, as one, the crowd breathed and sound came rushing back. Bart voiced his approval once more. The Brother wearing the special robe said a few more words, made the sign of the cross over the townspeople, and told them to "Go in Peace."

Then Simon spoke up, "We, the Poor Brothers, hope you have been blessed by our Christmas Nativity. We hope from now on at Christmastime you will be able to picture in your mind that wonderful night Jesus was born. Remember he is our Emmanuel, which means 'God with us.'

"As you leave for your homes, we want to sing you one last song. Children, get ready to give us your best animal sounds!"

Simon untied a little drum from his waist and started a lively beat. Mundo's flute joined in. It was a popular tune called "The Friendly Beasts." Mundo sang out, his voice as pure and steady as his flute:

Jesus our brother kind and good
Was humbly born in a stable of wood
And the friendly beasts around him stood
Jesus our brother kind and good

Mundo went back to playing. Now the children hopped up and down, for they knew what was coming.

Francesco and the Poor Brothers stamped their feet to the beat and smiled as they sang the next verse:

"I" said the donkey shaggy and brown
I carried his mother up hill and down
I carried him safely to Bethlehem town
"I" said the donkey shaggy and brown

"Hee haw! Hee haw!" shouted the children.

And "I" said the ox all white and red
I gave him my manger for a bed
I gave him my hay for to pillow his head
"I" said the ox all white and red

"Moo, Moo!" cried the children.

"I" said the sheep with a curly horn
I gave him my wool for his blanket warm
And he wore my coat on that Christmas morn
"I" said the sheep with a curly horn

"Baa, Baa!" shouted Bart and the children together. And so it went until the final verse:

Thus every beast remembering it well
In the stable dark was so proud to tell
Of the gifts that they gave Emmanuel
The gifts that they gave Emmanuel

As the song ended, the people could not contain themselves. They hugged each other, and shouts of "Merry Christmas!" filled the air. Then one by one they relit their candles, picked up their lanterns, and made their way back down the mountainside. Bart watched them go. For a long time the sound of their singing rose like echoes through the mountain air.

"I" said the donkey shaggy and brown . . .

Mundo began preparing for the trip back home. Just when Bart was feeling sorry it was all over, Simon walked up with another Brother at his side. It was Francesco.

"Mundo—bless you for bringing your animal friends and your talents to help us," said Francesco.

"It was . . . it was the most wonderful thing I have ever been a part of. Thank you for including me," said Mundo, bowing his head with respect.

"You are a good shepherd, my son," said Francesco. Bart *baa-ed* loudly in agreement.

Francesco chuckled. "And you are a special sheep," he said, patting Bart on the head. Then he looked at Violeta, Jaco, and Bart in turn. "Thank you all for being part of our celebration of the Nativity—the birth of Jesus. You have given praise and honor to our Lord on Christmas Eve."

He turned back to Mundo. "Speaking of being honored, our friend Lord Giovanni was here tonight. He has invited you to come to Greccio castle tomorrow to share the Christmas Day meal. That is, unless you have to go home?"

Mundo looked like he couldn't believe what he was hearing.

"I, uh, I can go, yes, of course. What about the Poor Brothers and you, Brother Francesco?" he asked.

"Lord Giovanni knows we prefer to eat a simple Christmas supper here with our poor guests. Although he did insist on sending us some almond honey cakes as a special thank-you. Now, go to the castle stables this evening and the stablemaster will have a place for your animals, and for you."

Then Francesco smiled. "Peace and goodwill to you, my son. And farewell," he said.

"Peace and goodwill to you, Brother Francesco, and to you, Simon. I will never forget this night as long as I live," said Mundo.

As Francesco turned and left, Bart felt an urge to follow him. Then Mundo's hand was on his back. "Stay here, boyo," said Mundo. Bart watched Poverello walking away, and *baa*-ed his goodbye.

A short while later, Mundo had the animals tied together and held a small lamp from his pack in one hand. The little procession of shepherd, ox, donkey and sheep made their way down the trail, onto the main road and into the town. The castle walls were lit with torches visible from far away. At the front of the castle the street widened out into a town square. Two of the castle towers made up one side of the square. A guard stood in front of a tall arched gateway between the towers. Mundo walked up and gave the guard Lord Giovanni's message, and he let them all pass. Through the arch was a big courtyard with stables on two sides. Mundo soon found the stablemaster.

"Ah, the shepherd boy who plays so beautifully, and the beasts from the Nativity! Merry Christmas to you!" said the stablemaster. He led them into one of the stables and down a long row of stalls. Bart heard the rustling sound of large animals. In the dim light he made out here the gleam of a dark eye and there the curve of a proud neck. He heard deep throaty rumbles, the stamp of a hoof, and the swish of silky manes and tails. At the end of the row were two empty stalls. "We will put the donkey and the ox here. I will send a stablehand to feed and water them."

When Jaco and Violet were settled, the stablemaster led Mundo and Bart back to the courtyard and into the other stable building. "We are very full with guests who came to see the Poor Brothers' Nativity. But here is a stall for the sheep, and the loft above it has fresh straw and blankets for your bed. I will send you some food. You must be quite hungry."

The stablemaster left, and a few minutes later, a young boy appeared with a basket in his hands. That night Bart munched on some very fine hay while Mundo took his spoon from his waist pouch and dug into a bread bowl filled with meat stew. He had a jug of water mixed with wine to drink.

Afterward, as Mundo slept soundly in the loft above, Bart chewed his cud and thought of everything that happened. He was so pleased to be part of something new at Christmastime. Now he understood honor and praise. But he was still not sure about love and belonging. How was love a gift? And besides his wool, what gift could a little lamb give to anyone?

Chapter Eleven

On Christmas morning, after getting some water and hay for Bart, Mundo went to check on Violeta and Jaco. When he came back, he said to Bart, "I just spoke to the stableboy and he said Lord Giovanni has a special Christmas treat for all the animals in the stables—a warm mash of oats! That's usually only given to the lord's horses. You're gonna like that, boyo. Now be good, stay put, and enjoy your Christmas treat. I'll be back in a couple of hours."

Mundo found the stablemaster, and they made their way out of the stable and across the stone courtyard to another entrance between two more towers. The massive door in the wall was closed, but the guard there opened a regular-sized door built into the larger one. They stepped through into a second courtyard, nearly as big as the first. In the center of it a fire blazed in a large firepot. Work-rooms and a building smelling like a kitchen surrounded the courtyard.

At a table off to one side, people came and went. Men, women, and a few children all had a certain thinness in their faces. They were people familiar with hunger and need. Behind the table were three servants wearing the green and blue uniform of Lord Giovanni's house. The first man noted their names in a book. The second man handed each person or family bundles of firewood. The third servant, a woman, poured something warm from a large pot into the tin cups the people carried tied to their waists. "Please come back an hour before sunset for your Christmas dinner. Merry Christmas from Lord Giovanni and his household," she said, smiling at each of them.

"Lord Giovanni has always done his Christian duty and given alms—like food and firewood—to the poor at Christmastime," said the stablemaster. "But he has become more generous these days." The stablemaster leaned close to Mundo. "People say his friendship with Brother Francesco has a lot to do with that."

They walked across the courtyard to a wall on the other side where another guard asked Mundo his name. "Yes, the shepherd boy from the Nativity. Wait here," he said. The stablemaster nodded at Mundo and left. Very soon, another servant arrived to show Mundo indoors. They stepped into an entrance hallway then through wide double doors, into the biggest feast Mundo ever saw.

The great room of the castle held more people than lived in the entire Grange settlement. Wreaths and boughs of evergreens, holly, and mistletoe were strung along the walls. Three fireplaces blazed. The servant led Mundo to a table near the back. It was set with a fine white tablecloth, wooden plates and bowls and napkins. Mundo sat near the end of the table. To his right was a hammered copper bowl filled with water for washing fingers between servings. Platters heaped with food filled the middle of the table. The fellow sitting next to Mundo on the bench introduced himself.

"Welcome, shepherd. My name is Marco, and this is my wife, Maria. We are winemakers who work in Lord Giovanni's household. Across from you are my sister Bela and her husband, Matteo, and their three children. They are basket makers from Rieti Valley." Mundo told them his name and gave a little bow of his head to each adult, and then to the children. There was a boy aged about four, one about ten, and a girl of twelve or thirteen, who blushed very prettily.

"They were fortunate to be visiting us for Christmas, and got to see the Nativity last evening," said Marco. "My niece Olivia was just wondering if you were a real shepherd, and now you appear . . ."

At that moment someone called for silence, and the room quieted. All eyes turned to the front of the room, where the head table sat on a long stage raised about two feet off the floor. The people sitting there facing the rest of the room wore fine clothes of deep, rich shades. There were colorful patterns of vines and leaves and flowers sewn on them. Mundo could see glints of gold and silver thread, and thought he spotted jeweled rings and necklaces.

Then a man at the table stood, and everyone in the hall got quickly to their feet. The man looked to be a little older than Mundo's uncle and was dressed in a pale linen shirt and a plain tunic of dark green wool. His only jewelry was a large ring on one hand. Among the group of men and women decked out in silk and jewels, he seemed to be a partridge among peacocks. But something about the way he stood, his broad shoulders and his sharp gaze, said something different. Not a partridge, then. More like a falcon.

"As Lord of Greccio, I welcome you all to share our Christmas feast," he said, in a voice that carried to the far corners of the room. "It has been a year of blessings. We have had peace with our neighbors. Yes, there was a cruel winter, and we lost many who are dear to us, but it was followed by a glorious spring, summer, and fall. Because of that and thanks to everyone's hard work, we have a plentiful harvest to get us through the winter.

"And then last evening, something extraordinary took place. Brother Francesco and the Poor Brothers gave us a glimpse of the miracle that took place in the Holy Land. They brought the story of Christmas to life in a brand-new way. Every year from now on, I vow we in Greccio will celebrate Christmas Eve with a Nativity. We will have real beasts and sing carols about Christmas. When people think of Greccio, they will think of the Babe of Bethlehem!

"I would like to thank our Grange settlement for sending us their animals, and their talented shepherd. Mundo, please come up here."

Mundo's mouth opened, then quickly snapped shut. He took a deep breath, got up, and walked up to the head table, where he made a pretty decent bow.

"Mundo, I know your Uncle Vin and Aunt Lina, and I knew your grandfather, Bernardo. He had a shining spirit. You remind me of him. I am also impressed by your flute playing and singing. And getting your lamb to bleat at just the right moments—as if he understood Brother Francesco and was saying an 'Amen.' Quite wonderful! Would you agree to lend us your animals and your talents every Christmas from now on?"

"Yes, my lord," said Mundo, who looked scared and thrilled at the same time.

"That's wonderful," said Lord Giovanni. "My thanks to you and to your village. Now hold on," said Lord Giovanni as Mundo began to turn away. "There's something I want to give you." He held out a blue velvet bag. "I'm sure you will know who it's for. Go ahead and show everyone what it is."

Mundo upended the bag. Then grinning ear to ear, he held up the gift for all the guests to see. There was laughter and a few cheers. "Thank you, sir," said Mundo. "You're welcome, son," said Lord Giovanni. "Before you leave, go see the steward. I have a Christmas present for the Grangers." Then he leaned forward and whispered in Mundo's ear, "It's oranges from Sicily. I know you will make sure they all get one."

"Yes, sir," said Mundo. He bowed politely and returned to his table. A bishop gave the blessing, and everyone sat and began to pass food around.

Mundo was again the center of attention. The children of the basket maker asked him lots of questions—about how he learned to play his flute, about his animals, about being a shepherd. Finally, Marco chuckled and said, "Now let the boy eat. He is missing some of the best dishes. Here, Mundo, taste this fish—it's in a lemon sauce. You children tell Mundo something about yourselves now."

"We have a donkey," said ten-year-old Paolo.

"And a few chickens, of course," added Olivia.

"And some hives of bees who live in the bee baskets we made for them," said Paolo.

"Beehives! Now that's something that would work well at the Grange," said Mundo. "We have orchards and gardens. There's plenty of flowers for bees. And it sure beats having to find a wild hive to get some honey."

Mundo kept being offered new dishes of food and he turned nothing down. "A few years ago," said Marco, "this feast would have had a special dish of baked songbird. You know, larks, sparrows, goldfinches, and the like. Very popular around here. But Lord Giovanni heard that Brother Francesco preaches to the little birds. He knows they are very close to Poverello's heart. So, Lord Giovanni stopped serving that dish out of respect for Brother Francesco. Now he won't even let the little birds be hunted on his land."

"I'm glad about that," said Olivia. "What do you think of the sweet cakes, Mundo? They are made with chestnut flour."

"They're delicious," said Mundo. "I didn't know you could make so many things out of chestnuts. My grandfather loved them. He started planting chestnut trees around the Grange land when he was a young man. Two years ago, the first ones he planted finally started producing nuts. He was thrilled he lived to see it."

Just then the sound of plucked strings cut through the chatter. Mundo's head whipped around, looking for the minstrels. There they were in the far corner, one playing the strings of a lute, one a small harp, and the third a tambourine. Their fingers flowed over the strings without any effort. Their feet and heads kept time to the music, and their ears kept the music blending in a tuneful way. While most people kept on eating and talking, Mundo's attention was now entirely on the musicians. He thought they all looked like they were related. A family of musicians?

At one point the oldest looking of the three, the lyre player, put down his instrument and picked up another. "Look at that, I think that's a fiddle," said Mundo to Paolo and Olivia. "I've never seen one of those before. These minstrels are really good."

"You are a pretty good musician yourself," said Olivia.

"I would love to learn how to play as well as you do," said Paolo.

"Gee, thanks," said Mundo. "I'd be glad to help you learn." He then got so wrapped up in the music he didn't notice the basket maker and his wife were preparing to leave until the final note of the song ended.

"We have to get going so we can make it home by nightfall. It was good to meet you, Mundo," said Matteo.

"Merry Christmas to you and your family," said Bela.

"And to yours," said Mundo.

"Merry Christmas, Mundo," said Olivia. "Merry Christmas and goodbye," said Paolo. Their little brother just waved shyly.

The minstrels were starting another song. The winemaker Marco turned to Mundo. "Don't feel you have to leave as well. Stay and listen to the music. Then you can go find the steward."

"Thank you," said Mundo. "This has been a Christmas I will never forget."

In the stable, Bart finished his hay, and was daydreaming about the oats Mundo told him were coming. In the stall next to him, a young donkey poked his head over the wall between them.

"Hello. My name is Tonio."

"My name is Bart. Nice to meet you, Tonio," replied the lamb. "Do you belong to Lord Giovanni?"

"Oh no," said Tonio. "I belong to a family who are visiting for Christmas. They put me up here."

"My master is Mundo the shepherd," said Bart, proudly. "We live not far from here and came to Greccio town because Poverello asked us to be part of the Christmas Eve Nativity. Now I'm just waiting for my Christmas oats while Mundo eats supper at the castle."

"My master's family was very excited about coming to see the Nativity. What was it like?"

"Well," said Bart. "I really should start at the beginning." Bart told him the whole story about meeting the lark and the hare and the wolf and Poverello coming past their village. The donkey was a good listener.

"What a wonderful story," he said. "I never knew sheep were so smart."

Bart beamed. "You are kind," he said. "In fact, you remind me of a friend of mine. Do you like your human family?"

"Oh, yes, they are a good family. The children like to lie on my back. I even let them put straw hats on my head. I carried the little one and his mom most of the way here from the valley. But mainly I work with my master. He makes baskets and I carry them to market. If it weren't for him, I probably wouldn't be alive today to speak with you."

"Tell me about that," said Bart. "I like to hear stories."

"I was born not far from here," said the donkey. "I was still very young the day some men came and took me from my mother. They loaded me down with all sorts of heavy things. I had to carry the load all day long. On the third day of doing this I came up lame. The men were moving quickly, with loaded mules and horses and they didn't care about one lame donkey. So they left me behind at an inn and kept going. The innkeeper and another man came to look me over. I didn't like the other man, he smelled of blood and dead things. I was afraid of him—I think he only wanted me for my hide. But he left without taking me, thank goodness.

"The next day my master showed up. He came over and spoke softly to me and patted me and looked me up and down. Then he spoke to the innkeeper and gave him some coins and put some medicine on my sore foot. A few days later when I could walk a little better, he led me away to a little stall behind a cottage where he was staying. He fed me and brushed me and nursed my foot until I healed, which took a few weeks. Then one day we walked all the way back to Rieti and I met his wife and kids. I learned to carry things little by little, more and more, and now I am strong enough to carry as much as any donkey! Stronger, even!"

"I believe it. You certainly are a fine, healthy-looking donkey," Bart replied. "You know, your story sounds familiar, like one I've heard before."

At that moment, Paolo and Olivia came running up. Their father Matteo was right behind them.

"Hello, Tonio! How are you, boy?" said Paolo, opening the stall door. He and his sister fussed over him as their father put on his halter and led him out. Marco spoke in a calm, low voice to the donkey as he placed a wool felt pad on his back and tied some bundles to his sides.

"Look, Olivia," said Paolo. "It's the sheep who was in the Nativity. It's Mundo's sheep!"

"Yes, you're right," said Olivia. "I recognize those black and white ears. Hey there, boy!" she said, leaning over the stall door to pet Bart on the head.

"Okay, let's go, kids," said Matteo. "Your mom and brother are waiting."

"Goodbye, Bart," said Tonio as he was led away.

Bart was thinking hard. "Tonio, wait!" he said suddenly. He rose on his hind legs, but could only get his nose over the door of the stall. The sound of the children's chatter was getting fainter. "TONIO! WHAT WAS YOUR MOTHER'S NAME!?" he shouted as loudly as he could.

Bart held his breath, listening. He wasn't sure if the donkey had heard him.

From a distance the reply floated back to him. "It was Violeta!"

Then there was silence. They were gone.

Chapter Twelve

Bart began pacing in his stall, back and forth. He was now sure he had just been talking to Violeta's son, even though his name was Tonio, not Seymour. But what to do with this stunning news?

Just then a stableboy entered, whistling a Christmas song. He had steaming buckets in his hands and began pouring something into each stall's feed trough. From the delicious aroma it must be the promised warm oat mash.

Bart knew he had to make a decision fast. Mundo told him to stay put and enjoy his Christmas mash until he returned. On the other hand, Tonio was getting farther and farther away every second. Farther from him, and farther from Violeta.

The beginnings of a plan came into his head. It would mean disappointing Mundo after so many weeks of behaving well, and that made him sad. It would also mean not getting to eat his mash. He really didn't want to disappoint Mundo or miss his oat mash. But more important to him was knowing the truth, for Violeta's sake.

The whistling stableboy dumped some mash into the trough of the stall opposite Bart's and moved on down to the next one. Soon he would reach the last stall at the end of the stable and would switch to Bart's side.

The first part of Bart's plan was the toughest. Getting out of the stall. He checked the stall door for a latch he could nudge open. But it was locked from the outside. That meant he would have to jump. But it was nearly twice as high as he was tall. He had never cleared something that high, and he didn't have much room to run. Could he do it?

Bart couldn't wait any longer. He closed his eyes and took some deep breaths. In his mind he could hear Ginevra's voice. "You can jump as high as I can, Bart. Jump Bart! NOW!" He backed up and charged right at the stall door. At just the right moment, instinct and need lifted him on his back legs. Next thing he knew he was somehow over the stall door, stumbling onto his front knees. "Hey, Hey!" the stableboy shouted from the other end of the aisle. Bart was up in a flash and dashing toward the courtyard.

In the bright light of the courtyard, he blinked twice then headed for the main gate, which stood open. He ran past the guards, who were facing the street and didn't see him until it was too late. He ran across the square and paused to look down the road in both directions, but there was no sign of the family and Tonio.

"Where did they GO!" he bleated out loud.

"Where did *who* go, little lamb?" said a voice overhead. Bart looked up and saw a bird fly over and land on a nearby tree.

"Mr. Lark, is that you?"

"Yes, yes, it is."

"I'm searching for a family with a donkey. I have to find them for a friend!"

"I just flew over a donkey and some humans who were heading south. That way, little lamb!"

"Thank you!" said Bart and took off, just as the stable-boy came through the gate yelling, "Stop that lamb!"

The road started out wide but quickly narrowed. Bart stayed in the center as much as he could, dodging around two people in his way. Very quickly the wall-to-wall houses thinned out and the road began to curve. Bart couldn't hear anyone behind him but he didn't slow. He kept peering down the road, expecting to see Tonio—he couldn't be that much farther ahead.

RahrahRAH! A dog sprung from behind a building. Bart was startled and darted to the side. The dog angled down as if to cut him off and grab him. Bart sized him up in an instant: young, overeager, as tall as Bart but not as heavy. "Baaack off!" Bart shouted, as he ran. The dog ignored the warning and kept coming. At the last minute Bart turned his body, lowered his head, and swung it low to high. It caught the hound just under his forearm. The dog flew into the air and landed with a surprised yelp. Bart didn't even look back. After battling a wolf, he was not going to let one pesky pup stop him.

He came around a curve and there was the family right in front of him. Matteo was leading Tonio. His wife Bela walked next to the donkey. The littlest boy was up on Tonio's back and Olivia and Paolo walked behind him.

"Tonio! Tonio!" cried Bart.

"Look, it's that sheep from the stables! It's Mundo's sheep!" cried Paolo.

"What's he doing here?" said Matteo.

"Where's Mundo?" said Olivia, looking around.

"Tonio! Seymour! You have to come with me," Bart said, out of breath. "I know where your mother is!"

The donkey halted in surprise. "I haven't been called Seymour since I was a colt. What do you mean? Where is my mother?" asked Tonio.

"She was the donkey in the Nativity last night. She's in the stables at the castle we just left. You were so close to each other and didn't know it. It would mean the world to her to see you again."

The little family watched the sheep baaing and the donkey braying back to him.

"I think they must be talking," said Paolo to his sister.

"I want to come with you but I can't abandon my family," said Tonio.

"I'll take care of that," said Bart. "I have a plan."

"We can't just leave him here, we have to return him, Father," said Olivia.

Matteo sighed. "Yes. It wouldn't be right to leave him here. You two try to catch him."

But Bart was ready for them and led Paolo and Olivia around in circles. After a few minutes of that, Matteo said, "That's not working, so let's try to herd him back. Look, now he is going in the right direction!"

The family turned around and began to drive Bart in front of them. "Shoo, shoo, back to the stable," said Olivia, waving her arms.

Bart trotted in front of them without getting close enough to be caught. He retraced his steps to the castle. A boy and a girl leaning out of a window in a row of houses laughed and pointed.

"Look, a whole family herding one sheep!" said the boy.

"No, it's a sheep leading a whole family and their donkey," said the girl.

When Bart reached the square in front of the castle walls, he called out to Tonio. "Follow me and I'll bring you to her." Then he began to run. If he stopped now everything would be lost.

He ran between the guards as they moved to grab him. One nearly caught his back leg but he kicked free. He ran full-tilt to the stable on the other side of the courtyard where Violet and Jaco were staying.

"Bart, Bart!" It was Mundo, just coming through the entrance from the castle courtyard carrying two big sacks over his shoulders. But Bart didn't slow down.

"VIOLETA! VIOLETA!" he shouted as he ran down the stable's center aisle.

"What is it, dear child, what's the matter!" said Violeta.

"What's this all about?" said Jaco from the stall next to her.

"It's Seymour! I've found him, Violeta, your son Seymour. He's here!"

"Seymour? Here?" said Violeta in her breathy voice.

"Yes, in the courtyard, with a basket maker and his family and—"

Mundo dropped the bags and he and the stable hand ran toward Bart. This time he didn't have room to get away. Mundo caught him and started putting the rope halter on him.

"Have you gone crazy!?" said Mundo. "What were you thinking? I guess I will just have to keep you tied up. Come on now."

"Violeta!" said Bart as Mundo began to pull him away. "Seymour's here, just outside. He knows you're here but his family doesn't, and they must be holding him back. I'm sorry. I tried my best, Violeta."

No one expected what happened next. Bart heard something he had never heard before. It was a sound that stopped Mundo in his tracks. It was a sound so loud, everybody in the entire town of Greccio could hear it.

"SeeMORE! SeeMORE! SeeMORE!" Violeta brayed at the top of her lungs. "SeeMORE! SeeMORE! SeeMORE!"

"MoTHER! came an answering cry from the courtyard. Tonio pulled hard against his lead rope, trying to get to the stable, but Matteo shouted in surprise and planted his feet. Paolo and Olivia looked at each other, the same crazy thought dawning on both their faces. Then Tonio grew still as he felt the little boy on his back losing his balance.

Olivia leaped toward her little brother and swung him off the donkey's back. "Father!!" cried Olivia. "Tonio knows that donkey. Please let him go!"

"SeeMORE! SeeMORE!"

"I'm HERE!" cried Tonio.

"Let him go Father, please?" said Paolo. "It's Christmas!"

Their startled father stared at them for several seconds. Then he dropped the rope.

Immediately, the donkey ran into the stable and down the aisle, the little family trailing behind him.

He came right up to Violeta, who was still braying, although more softly now. He put his head over the stall door, and she did the same, and they stood there, nibbling each other's necks and braying softly to each other.

"My darling son," said Violeta, "it has been so long. Are you well?"

"Yes, Mama. I'm fine. I work hard for my basket maker and his family, and they take good care of me."

"Tell me how you came to them. I was sure the knights were taking you away to a far-off land and I would never see you again."

"I think they meant to take me to a battle, but here is what happened . . ." Then he told her what he told Bart, about being left at the inn and being rescued by Matteo.

The humans stood there watching the two donkeys, amazed. Then Mundo said, "I recognize your donkey now. I haven't seen him for three or four years, since he was a colt, but I know him. He's Violeta's son. His name is Seymour."

"He had no name when I bought him, so we named him Tonio," said Matteo.

"He knew!" said Paolo.

"Who did?" said his father.

"The sheep," said Olivia. "He knew Tonio was Violeta's son. That's why he escaped and found us. He brought us back so the two of them could see each other again. It wouldn't have happened otherwise."

"That's a nice story but it's nonsense, Olivia," said her father. "Ask Mundo. He's a shepherd. He knows what sheep are capable of."

Mundo was staring at Bart, who looked right back at him and tossed his head. Mundo blinked hard.

"With most sheep, I'd say you were right, sir," said Mundo. "But not this one. For one thing, he was singled out by Brother Francesco to be part of the Christmas Eve Nativity."

"They say Poverello can talk to the animals, and they can talk to him," said the stablehand, making the sign of the cross as he spoke.

"Mundo," said Bela. "I think your lamb is no ordinary lamb. And I think you are no ordinary shepherd."

"Mama, can we go visit Mundo at the Grange settlement?" said Paolo. "We could bring some of our baskets to trade. Mundo says they want to start some beehives. And that way Tonio, uh Seymour, and Violeta can see each other again. And we can see Mundo. He's going to teach me how to play the flute!"

Bela chuckled. "I think we could come visit Mundo in early spring when it starts to get warmer. As long as you've been working hard and behaving and your dad says it's okay," she said.

And so the little family got ready to leave again. The children patted Jaco, said goodbye to Violeta, and hugged Bart. "See you again soon, Mundo," they said.

The two oldest children turned and waved to him as they passed through the castle gate and out of view. Mundo waved back and was rewarded with a big smile and a blush from Olivia.

The stable hand helped Mundo arrange the two sacks of oranges across Jaco's back. Mundo put his bedroll on Violeta's back. He carried his flute and the present from Lord Giovanni in his pouch.

Then he tied the three animals together and led them through the gate, across the square and onto the main road going north.

It was difficult to talk to Violeta because he was behind her, so Bart spent the return trip thinking about everything that had happened. He hoped Mundo would not be too upset with him. He hated to think the boy might not trust him anymore. But if he had to do it all over again, he knew he would do the same thing.

An hour and a half later they were walking up the path to the Grange settlement. Bart heard some shouts and saw people in the village coming out of their doors. By the time Mundo put Jaco and Violeta in their stalls and took Bart's rope halter off, a dozen people were gathered around, all talking excitedly to Mundo.

"Bart!" said Ginevra, who came bounding up to him. "How was it, how was Christmas? Did you find out what you wanted to know?"

"Yes, I did, Ginevra. Poverello was there and he helped me see what it was all about. It was wonderful."

The rest of the flock was milling around Bart. Even Peco and Nana goat were there.

"Bart is a brave, true friend," said Violeta. "Because of him, I saw my son Seymour again, and I'm no longer sad wondering what happened to him. It is the nicest gift anyone could have given me."

"Well, I couldn't have done it without Ginevra," said Bart. "She believed in me before I believed in myself."

"Aw, shucks," said Ginevra happily.

"Listen up, everyone," said Jaco, taking charge. "This is big news. Violeta has her voice back. For those of you who haven't heard it yet, let me say, it's a doozy."

"Now, Jaco," said Violeta. "I've always had my voice; I was just afraid to use it. But I won't be anymore."

Uncle Vin's voice suddenly cut through all the excited chatter of humans and animals. "Everyone, quiet down. I know we are all glad to see Mundo after that wonderful Christmas Eve."

"I've brought oranges from Lord Giovanni for everyone, with his best Christmas wishes!" shouted Mundo.

There were cheers from the villagers.

"Yes, yes," said Uncle Vin. "The oranges are a very nice gift. But what is nicer is having our musical shepherd boy back home with us. We were half worried Lord Giovanni would steal you away. And then we would have to storm the castle to get you back," he said, and everyone laughed.

"So, tell us, Mundo. If you really want to be a minstrel—and I know you've thought about it—now is your chance. We could sell your grandfather's and your portion of the flock and some of mine as well and buy an apprenticeship. After six or seven years of learning you would be a minstrel, and a fine one, I'm sure. What do you think?"

Mundo's eyes were wide as he looked around him. He didn't say anything for a long moment.

"Uncle Vin, I am so honored and grateful you would do that for me. I know if I worked hard for many years I could become a decent minstrel one day. Like the ones who played at Lord Giovanni's Christmas banquet."

The Grangers were all very quiet now. Uncle Vin and Mundo looked at each other for a long minute in silence.

"But as nice as that might be," said Mundo. "I think— no, I believe, I'm meant to stay here in Greccio Grange. I didn't always know that, but now I do. I would miss not just all of you, but all the animals, and all this," he said, waving his hand around him. "I want to build up the flock, not see it sold off. I want to plant more chestnut trees and make chestnut flour and add some beehives so we have more things to fall back on when the crops don't do well. I want to play music when feast days come around and watch all my friends and family dancing and enjoying themselves.

"Okay, so I still want to travel to a few places and save up to buy a fiddle. But I don't want to play for strangers all the time, far away from home. And besides, Lord Giovanni has invited me to be part of the Nativity celebration every year. Just think of it! Christmas will never be the way it used to be. And on Christmas Eve I get to play music to honor—not just some lord or duke or king—but the greatest Lord of all, the King of kings!

"I hope that's okay with you, Uncle Vin."

"Of course, Mundo," said his uncle with a sigh. "We didn't want to see you go, but you deserved to have that choice. I've always known you had a gift for animals as well as music. You care for them and, more than that, you understand them. What I didn't realize until now was you have a lot of practical wisdom too. Chestnut trees and beehives, huh?"

"And one more thing," said Mundo. "Lord Giovanni gave me a gift." Mundo pulled out the blue velvet pouch. He emptied the contents into his hand and held up a braided leather cord. From it dangled a shiny, brass bell with silver trim. It was engraved with the image of the six towers of Greccio castle. He shook the bell hard, and it tinkled like a mountain brook.

High in the common pasture, a young hare stood up on her hind legs and gazed down on the little scene. On the mountain knee just above the road, a large gray wolf paused on his homeward journey to watch what was happening.

Mundo turned toward Bart. Gathered all around them now were the villagers and the whole flock. Jaco and Violeta looked on from their stalls.

"A good shepherd knows his flock, my grandfather used to say," Mundo said in a loud voice. "And every flock has a leader. The one who knows which way the wind is blowing. The one who is the first to know what's going to happen, who finds the path. The one the others follow. The *bellwether*.

"And I know just the wether this bell is meant for. Come here, Bart, you rascal!"

Bart trotted forward, black and white ears flopping. Mundo smiled at Bart, then knelt in front of him. Raising the bell for all to see, he carefully tied it around Bart's wooly neck. Then he wrapped his arms around him.

As Mundo hugged him, Bart heard birds singing. He looked up and saw a flock of larks circling above them. At that moment Bart felt like his heart had become a bird too, soaring high in the sky.

"You're always full of surprises, Bart, always ahead of me," Mundo said softly. "But now I will always know where to find you.

"*Merry Christmas*, my bellwether boyo!"

THE END

Courtesy: biografieonline.it

Who Is St. Francis?

This book was inspired by the life and legends of St. Francis of Assisi.

He was born and baptized Giovanni di Pietro di Bernardone in late 1181 or early 1182 but was called Francesco, which means "Frenchie." He was the son of a wealthy Italian cloth merchant. By the time he was in his late teens, he dressed elegantly, threw impressive parties, sang like a troubadour, and spoke French as well as he did Italian. Whenever Francis decided to do something, he did it in a big, bold way.

His family expected him to follow in his father's footsteps by becoming a merchant, but Francis wanted to be a knight. When he was a young man his family paid for expensive armor, a horse, and a squire for him. But as soon as he left to join up with an army, he fell ill and changed his mind. Even so, he kept having dreams and visions of a lovely, noble lady he was supposed to serve, just as any good knight would.

One day, he went inside a very old, decaying church on the edge of town. While he gazed at the image of Jesus painted on the cross above the altar, he heard the image telling him to "repair my house." He began camping out at the church. He took bundles of expensive cloth from the family business and sold them for repair money. He sang and begged for building stones.

Some townspeople started calling him a madman. His father was furious. When repeated beatings and even house imprisonment did not convince Francis to give up what he was doing, his father brought him before the local bishop and townspeople and demanded the repair money. Francis gave him the purse of money, then took off all his clothes and threw them at his father's feet. He declared that from then on, his only father was God, his Father in heaven.

Francis began to dress like a beggar. He became completely devoted to a noble ideal he called Lady Poverty. He gave away whatever he had to the poor and begged for his own food. He took care of lepers with horrible sores on their bodies. Wherever he went he preached about the goodness of God. Soon others began to join him, and that's how Francis' band of Poor Brothers was formed.

To the medieval church, which was struggling, Francis and his followers were like a breath of fresh air. The Poor Brothers were determined to imitate the earliest followers of Jesus: traveling around preaching the Good News, staying humble, bringing peace, and giving away their possessions to the poor. Every day they depended on God, not money, for their daily bread.

By 1223, the year of *A Bellwether Christmas*, hundreds of people decided to follow Francis's example of living a simple life and helping others. Franciscan friars and nuns soon numbered in the thousands and spread their practices throughout the church and Christian lands.

Francis loved nature. The sun, moon, and stars were his brothers and sisters. So were all God's creatures. There are many delightful stories of Francis speaking to animals. This book describes just a few of them. Remarkably, animals seemed to understand his love for them and were drawn to Francis as if to a brother.

Francis once gave a sermon to a flock of birds on the ground. Witnesses say the birds did not move until he dismissed them. He was especially fond of larks—plain, brown-and-white birds with beautiful voices that reminded him of nuns. A wild hare jumped into his lap three times after being released from a snare.

Perhaps the most amazing story of all is the Wolf of Gubbio. Did it really happen? We don't know for sure; but tradition says that after Francis tamed the beast, the wolf went from home to home being fed by the townspeople for two years. When he died, the residents of Gubbio gave him a solemn burial and built a church named after St. Francis on that site. In 1872, when the church in Gubbio, Italy, was being renovated, workers lifted a stone slab. There lay a large skeleton of a wolf several centuries old!

When Francis arrived in Greccio, Italy, which is not far from his hometown of Assisi, he was thinking of what he had seen when he visited the Holy Land of the Bible. It gave him the idea of creating a living, breathing Nativity scene, and right then and there he set out to do it with his usual dramatic flair—with candlelight and singing, a mountain cave, donkey, ox, and a touching sermon about the Babe of Bethlehem. It was a huge and immediate success, and towns everywhere quickly began staging their own Nativity scenes. In Italy it is called a *presepio*, and elsewhere it is called a crèche, crib, or manger scene. Eight hundred years later it is still a beloved Christmas tradition.

Francis's health was never very good. He had stomach problems and recurring fevers, probably from malaria. His eyes hurt and he was losing his sight. Not long after he left Greccio, while praying alone near a mountain cave one evening, he had a vision of an angel with wings of fire. People who lived nearby say they saw the mountaintop lit as if by fiery flames in the middle of the night. From then until his death in 1226 at the age of forty-four, Francis carried wounds on his hands, feet, and side, the same wounds as Christ received on the cross, known as the Stigmata.

At dusk on the day Francis died, a flock of larks flew down low around the house where he lay dying, singing gloriously and swirling about for a long time.

If Francis were here today, he would urge people to help the poor and sick, especially at Christmas. He would tell them not to forget the lowly beasts, either. He once said if he met the emperor, he would beg him to command that grain be scattered on the roads at Christmas for the birds, especially "our sisters" the larks.

It's no wonder St. Francis is considered the patron saint of animals and the environment. If you love animals like he did, why not feed the wild birds at your home at Christmastime? That way a beloved saint's eight-century-old wish could become a brand-new tradition.

Afterword

A uthors can have a lot of love for their characters. But in my case, that is especially true. The characters are based on real animals I have loved.

My curly-haired son collected barnyard animals starting at the age of thirteen, until he had a little herd of five. When he left home as a young man, I was the one who ended up caring for them. I will tell you about them, and I think you will recognize which characters they inspired.

Sir Barton, a wether, was a very clever rascal and an escape artist. He attracted attention early on when he caused a commotion at the Ventura County Fair by letting himself and his fellow lambs out of their pen. I once watched him break into a little shed filled with hay and grain. First, he turned the key in the door handle with his mouth. Then he turned the door handle with his head. Then he pushed his nose through the crack in the door. Barton was always friendly and noticed everything. He knew his name and would trot over to me (he never walked) and ask for a back scratching. Like all sheep, loud noises and sudden moves and unfamiliar things could scare him, even when he was full grown. But he always stood up to dogs. Once, when Barton was about three, a very large young Anatolian Shepherd got too excited at meeting his first sheep and started to nip Barton's ears. Barton backed up, put his head down and flung the pup into the air. After that they became friends.

Lady Guinevere is a beautiful ewe who was Barton's best friend. She followed him anywhere. One day Barton opened their pen and Guinevere followed him up into the Santa Monica Mountains, which is coyote territory. Fortunately, my son soon discovered they were gone and ran full tilt until he found them. He called to them, and they followed him home. We learned how high a lamb could jump the day we tried to separate the two lambs. Guinevere jumped over a barn door more than twice her height to be with Barton. Even so, whenever he made her mad, she would throw her ears back, cock her head, and butt him hard.

Violet is a sweet and gentle donkey. My son asked us to rescue her from a wild herd being rounded up on a large tract of land near our home. For many months we thought Violet was mute. She did not bray any louder than a whisper. Then one day we heard this incredible noise. Either Violet's voice suddenly returned or she was now comfortable enough to use it.

Violet gave birth to her son Seymour about a week before we brought them both home. There is nothing cuter in this world than a baby donkey—all long legs and long ears. Seymour has been around humans his whole life, so unlike his mother, he has never been shy around people. He has grown into a big, strong donkey, but he still loves being petted.

Finally, there was Jim Dandy, a quarter horse my son rescued and trained. He was a laid-back, even-tempered older gelding. As the biggest animal, he always got the most food in the herd and naturally thought he was the herd boss. He chased the donkeys away if they tried to steal some of his food. But he always had a soft spot for his two little woolly friends, Barton and Guinevere. He would even let Barton walk right under him while he grazed.

Some of these friends are no longer with us, but I feel so blessed to have known them all, and I hope you feel blessed by the story I wrote about them.

Acknowledgments

The illustrations gracing this book are by Cortney Skinner (www.cortneyskinner.com), whose art I've admired since we worked together at a science fiction magazine years ago. He says, "I've always loved the crispness, power, and deceptive simplicity of medieval woodcuts. I wanted to create an approach to the illustrations that would evoke the feeling of medieval woodcuts yet add a modern touch for a contemporary audience." I could not have hoped for or imagined better results. Thank you, Cortney.

Next, I thank Gary Terashita, my patient, practical, and talented editor.

For their helpful feedback I thank my first-draft readers Pamela Hinckley and Jeannine Isbell, and junior readers Sarah Lucas, and Emily Gilbert.

I also thank my husband, Michael, for wholeheartedly supporting and encouraging me as I wrote this book and for bringing his expertise to my aid when I needed it.

Most of all, I want to thank the Lord, who downloaded the entire story into my brain one afternoon at Christmastime, then taught me how to write it with my heart. Glory be to God!